Black for a Funeral

The Wronged Women's Co-operative: Book 7

T E SCOTT

Copyright © 2024 T E Scott

All rights reserved.

ISBN: 9798879790375

This book is dedicated to Fraser, my oldest son who is reading these books for the first time and will be excited to see his name right here. Fraser, please skip over the rude bits!

Chapter 1: Bernie

The newspaper cutting had been folded and refolded until it was starting to fall apart at the creases.

Mrs BUTE (nee Montgomery) Peacefully at home on Sunday, December 8th, 2012, Elizabeth (Betty), aged 58 years. Beloved mother of Joyce and Michael. Cremation at Hill House Cemetery on December 14th at 1pm. Family flowers only please.

"Short and to the point," Bernie Paterson said, nodding her approval. "I can't stand it when they waffle on in obituaries. Just a chance for the family to show what good little mourners they are."

"Quite right," Detective Inspector Macleod replied, pushing a cushion behind his back to prop himself up on the sofa. DI Macleod was tall, old enough that he was starting to stoop a little, and had a Highland accent that could break rocks. Bernie thought that he was one of the least incompetent police officers that she had met, which was the highest praise could offer.

"However, it doesn't really tell me anything about the dead woman. Or about why you brought me this clipping in the first place."

Macleod, who had arrived at Bernie's house only ten minutes before, was being unusually reticent. "I wasn't sure how to broach the subject. You see, I want to give you some employment."

Witch, Bernie's cat, chose that moment to jump up onto the inspector's knee and shove her bum in his face.

"She likes you," Bernie said, giving the creature a scratch under her chin.

"Lovely," Macleod said, giving Witch a gentle shove so that she was out of his personal space.

"That's the kettle boiled," Bernie said. "I'll get you that coffee." Although she was interested in the Inspector's offer of employment, she didn't want to seem too eager. Always keep the coppers on their toes, that was Bernie's motto. She hoped he wouldn't be too long. She had a weights class to fit in before picking Ewan up from school at three.

"Here you go," Bernie said, handing him a 'World's Best Auntie' mug.

"At Mary's house I always get offered a chocolate biscuit," Detective Inspector Macleod said, taking a sip of his black coffee.

"Not here," Bernie said sharply. "I used to get them for my son but my husband would always munch the lot. He doesn't steal my protein bites."

"Imagine that," Macleod replied. "Now, let me get to the point."

"You need my help?" Witch settled onto Bernie's lap and started making biscuits on her jeans.

The Inspector shrugged. "You might be a pain in the arse, but

8

you get things done."

"And you don't want to take this through official police channels."

Macleod stiffened at this. "It's not that I don't want to. I would bloody love to. But the problem is that the case is officially closed. There's not enough room in the budget to investigate the cases we have, let alone reopening one from the past that no one gives a crap about."

"No one except you."

"Exactly."

Happy to be needed, Bernie tucked her legs up underneath her and sipped from her cup. "Why don't you tell me the whole story?"

Macleod leaned back in the chair. "I was still a Detective Sergeant then, not long moved to CID, as it was still called at that time. I'd been working in Edinburgh, in Leith, doing the drug busts for a while. That was pretty soul-destroying, as you might imagine. Trying to help people that were so far beyond help they didn't know they were already dead-men-walking." He coughed. "Anyway, I wanted a change so I headed over this direction for a two-year post working out of the station in Invergryff. I've always liked it here, the right size of town to have just enough crime to keep the likes of me busy, but not so big you feel like you are fighting a losing battle. Anyway, one of my first cases here was the death of Mrs Bute."

"She was murdered?" Bernie asked.

Macleod's mouth twitched at the corner. "You're getting ahead of yourself. When I was called in it was just a possible suspicious death. Elizabeth Bute had been found dead at the foot of her stairs by her daughter, Joyce. We were waiting on the cause of death at that point. My superiors thought it was probably natural causes, but they sent me to take statements just in case."

"And?"

"And nothing. Turned out she had a well-documented heart condition. Death could have occurred at any moment. There was nothing to suggest foul play. No motive for anyone to want her dead. She didn't have any money, only a few thousand pounds in her estate. Lived in a council house."

"But something about it stayed with you?"

"It was her children," Macleod said, checking his watch and gulping down his coffee. "A son and a daughter. You know, over the years you see that people grieve in all sorts of ways. Some scream and shout, some go completely silent. And none of that is suspicious. Only, sometimes people are a bit too perfect. You know, the single tear down the cheek, the brave face pulled when you ask them about their relative. You can tell when people are faking it."

Bernie nodded. She might not have been the best at reading people, but she could well understand that Macleod's long career would give him the experience necessary to spot a fake. "Which of the children did you think was faking their grief?"

"Both of them. They were glad their mother was dead, no

matter what they said."

Bernie tapped her fingernail against her top teeth. "Maybe the mother was just a horrible person. I mean, we like to think that all families are happy, but it's not true. Maybe she was a total horror and they were happy to see the back of her."

"You might have been right on that one. Except for the stepdaughter."

"There was a stepdaughter?"

"Yes. Much younger than the other two, barely out of her teens. Her name was Katie. Father was out of the picture long before. And this girl was genuinely upset at the loss of the woman. I tried to talk to her, but she wouldn't say anything to me. Skinny little thing, shaking all over. I reckon she was scared stiff."

"Scared? Of what?"

"The other two."

Macleod dropped his gaze to the laminate floor.

"And you just left her there?" Bernie said, pursing her lips.

"You don't need to take that tone," Macleod replied. "What other choice did I have? Officially, there had been no crime committed. But I was worried about her. I got in touch with the Social Work department, got them to step in for me, suggested she might be a vulnerable adult. But by the time they went to see them a week later, the three of them had moved out."

11

"Where did they go?"

"No idea. No one knew a forwarding address. I tried to search for them at the time, but the case was already closed, so it was deemed a waste of resources."

"Police corruption," Bernie sniffed.

Macleod actually laughed aloud. "Oh come on, you know it's not like that. Just lack of resources, not enough bodies, all the usual stuff. When the force gets it wrong – and it does happen, even I'll admit it – nine times out of ten it is neglect, not abuse. Understand?"

Bernie decided not to answer that one.

The Inspector sat down his empty cup on the table. "I'll send you over everything I've got. Obviously you can't access the official files, but I can give you all my personal notes. I don't have to tell you that this is very much off the record. I just… I want to know that that kid is okay. And if you can find evidence that her brother and sister killed the mother… well, that would be the icing on the cake."

"Why now?" Bernie asked when they were at the front door. "Why do you want to look at this all of a sudden if it was ten years ago?"

"Nothing much gets past you, does it?"

"Nothing at all," she replied, folding her arms. There was a moment of silence, but Bernie knew the inspector would cave.

He did. "I received a letter three days ago. That in itself is a bit of an event nowadays, isn't it? A handwritten letter from Mrs Volk, who used to be Mrs Bute's next-door neighbour. I'll get a copy of the letter for you, but it basically said that Mrs Bute had been unlawfully killed and that the police had missed it at the time."

"Wow."

"Yeah. It was a bit of a shocker, as you might expect."

"So you went to talk to Mrs Volk?"

"I did. Only there's no such person. I checked out the address and there was a new couple there. The lady that had lived there before, her name was Wilson and she's been dead for three years. There's no record of a Mrs Volk in the whole of Renfrewshire. I checked."

Bernie frowned, thinking this over. "Someone wants you to reopen the case by pretending to be a neighbour."

"Correct. But there's no case to reopen. We have no evidence to look at, no place to start."

"You could exhume the body," Bernie said. "I'm sure I've seen that happen on the telly."

Macleod laughed. "It's not that easy. Check the obituary. Mrs Bute was cremated as soon as her body was released to her children. There wasn't even a post-mortem as a doctor had seen her in the week before her death. The house has changed hands twice since then and any physical evidence is long gone."

"Sounds like a lost cause," Bernie said, although her mouth

quirked up into a smile. She had to admit, the whole story was intriguing. And she liked the idea of getting a conviction where the police service had failed. Yes, she liked that a lot.

"I can only pay you your standard consultancy rates," Macleod warned, buttoning up his coat. "I've fudged the budget so it's coming out of 'community policing'. But if you get anywhere with this case you'll be our top civilian investigators, and I'll make sure everyone knows it. You'll be fighting off clients."

Bernie knew she was being flattered, but she still held out her hand. "It's a deal."

Chapter 2: Liz

Liz Okoro was trying her third baby class of the month. So far, it was going significantly better than the other two. For one thing, no one had thrown up on her shoes. And for another, she wasn't the oldest person there by a decade. The problem was that she was not a first time mum, like most of the other parents who went to these things. With a twelve year old son at home, she didn't need tips on which nappies to use or how to treat teething gums. What she was looking for, ideally, were some friends.

It had become clear to Liz over the past year that apart from Mary and Bernie, she was short on the friends' quota. Most of her university pals had moved on to London or further afield, and the people she knew from her old job didn't seem to be much interested in her now that she was no longer in finance. It turned out they had been 'networking' rather than making actual friends.

And now that she had Isioma and was only working part-time for the WWC, Liz was longing for someone to meet up with for a cuppa and a chat. For a while, Mary had fulfilled that role, but the problem was they always ended up talking about WWC business. Work life and home life were becoming a bit too interconnected.

Isioma let out a gurgle and drooled down her chin. Liz leaned over the buggy and wiped her clean. The small side room just off the library was filling up and she lifted the baby onto her knee. Only half an hour of nursery rhymes to sit through, then the moment everyone was really there for: a chat with the other mums.

Feeling like the new kid at school, Liz sidled up to a group of three women who were around her age.

"This is a nice class," Liz said to the one nearest her, a lady with East Asian features and glittery nail polish.

"Not as good as the one in the church hall on Clyde Street," the woman replied with a smile. "You get tea and biscuits at that one."

"That sounds great, I'll have to look it up," Liz said, meaning what she said. A hot cup of tea was not something to be sniffed at when you had a small child. "Would you like to –"

Just at that moment, the woman with the pretty nails sniffed. "Whoops, I think we need a quick change," she said and swept up her child and hurried off to look for a bathroom.

Thwarted in her first attempt to befriend someone, Liz watched Isioma crawl across the floor and tried to stop her from sucking on shoelaces, pram wheels and rugs, in that order.

"Hello," a thin woman said, walking over to Liz with a wriggling male toddler under one arm. She was white with dyed red hair that was showing darker roots.

"Hi," Liz said, offering a smile.

"I'm Fiona Duncan. This is Marco."

"He's a sweetie," Liz said, while watching the little lad break free from his mum and start kicking a stand of postcards.

"So is yours. What's her name?"

"Isioma," Liz said proudly, watching her baby chew on her thumb. "This is my first time here."

"It's not too bad," Fiona said. "Except they got all religious at Christmas time. Started talking about Jesus and stuff. I didn't think it was very inclusive, you know?"

Liz shrugged. Despite being dragged to church as a child, she was largely agnostic, but she didn't think it was too 'out there' to mention Jesus on what was, technically, his birthday. But then again, she wanted to seem friendly, so she left the subject well alone.

"Did Marco like the nursery rhymes?"

"Yeah, I guess," Fiona said. "Apart from all the misogynistic ones. And that Ally Bally thing is just propaganda for sugar." She seemed distracted and in no mood to watch what her son was up to. Cute little Marco was currently terrorizing one of the librarians by licking the counter.

"You're um… you're that private investigator, aren't you?" Fiona said suddenly.

Liz stiffened. "I work for an investigation firm, yes."

"And what does that mean? Exactly."

"Just what it sounds like," Liz said, her heart sinking. "As a business we do investigations and research into issues that other people need help with. We take on private cases. All sorts of things, from lost jewellery to actual crimes. Stuff the police aren't interested in, or don't have time for."

"Missing persons?"

"Yes. We've done a few of them."

"And do you always find them? And bring them home?"

Liz sighed. She thought she had been making a new friend, but clearly the woman had a different agenda. "No, not always. If we explore every avenue we can and we don't come up with anything, then we tell that to the client."

"And they still have to pay you?"

"Yes. We've done the work, after all."

The other woman chewed her lip. "That makes sense I guess. How much is it?"

"That depends. I can't really say unless I know the details."

"Right." Fiona looked across to the window, staring out at the rain.

"Why don't you tell me who's missing?"

Belatedly, Fiona realised that her son was over on the other side of the building. By the time she had retrieved him, she seemed to have made up her mind.

"It's my partner. Marco's dad. I want you to do that thing. I mean, what you said. Investigate him."

Liz nodded. Bernie had taught her never to turn down a client, no matter how strange the situation. "All right. But with missing people we generally advise you to speak to the police first."

"I tried them," Fiona said, making a sour face. "They were no use."

"Well, they won't start looking for an adult unless it's been twenty-four hours, not unless there's a reason to think them especially vulnerable. How long has your husband been missing?"

"Eighteen months."

Chapter 3: Mary

It was a week until Valentine's Day and Mary Plunkett was having a crisis of faith. Last year, she and Walker hadn't been going out that long and a silly card and some chocolates had been enough to do the trick. This year, however, she had wanted to get him something a bit more special.

"I don't think his mouth is like that," her daughter Vikki said, tilting her head to one side. "And his nose looks kind of weird."

"Yeah, it looked better on the screen," Mary said, examining the framed print another time. "I'm not too sure about the background."

"Is it meant to be the desert?"

"No, it's supposed to be Mars. I think. Because we're astronauts, see?" She sighed. The watercolour had promised 'your photo transformed into avatars' and 'be your favourite superheroes'. What had arrived was a drawing of her and Walker wearing capes and standing on something that if you squinted, might just be an alien landscape.

"And wouldn't your heads explode without any air?"

"All right, I'm putting it away until Valentine's Day."

"I still think you should get something else." Vikki was ten years old going on twenty-five. She had told her mum that according to social media, what men really wanted was someone to feel their pecs and talk to them about the Roman Empire.

Mary had laughed at that, then made a note in her diary just in case. This was only her second long-term relationship, so she wasn't going to turn down any tips, no matter the source.

"Right, I'd better make some lunch," Mary said, checking the time. "I'm afraid it's beans on toast again."

Vikki stuck out her tongue.

"I know," Mary said. "It's not very exciting but you can have a bit of fruit after."

"I thought we were getting takeaway?"

"We're on a health kick. Remember when we went vegetarian for November?" Mary said.

"Aye, except for chicken nuggets."

"Except for chicken nuggets, obviously. Well, we might be doing a few more veggie meals this month."

Vikki sighed like an old woman. "Are we skint again?"

"Not exactly, but Johnny has just started violin lessons –"

"I can't believe you let him play that thing."

"It's good for his brain. And I bought you all earplugs. Anyway, my point is that by the time I've paid for all the extra stuff you guys love doing – music lessons, sports classes, toddler art club – well, it doesn't leave all that much leftover."

"So we're skint."

Mary kissed her on the forehead. "A bit. But only because we're doing so many fun things. And don't worry, all the bills are still getting paid, we just might have to cut back a bit. No cinema trips, that sort of thing. We'll do long walks on the beach, picnics in the park, stuff we can do for free."

"The beach? Lauren hates sand and Johnny always falls over and has a tantrum that the sea is so wet. And as for Peter and that thing with the crab –"

Mary's smile turned into something of a grimace. "We'll manage."

Vikki snuggled into her side. "You could do more work for Scary Bernie. I know she's been asking you to."

"Do you? You haven't been listening in to mum's conversations again, have you?" Mary gave her a tickle in the ribs.

"Maybe. I know she said you could do more hours if you wanted to."

Mary rubbed her chin. Some things were difficult to explain, especially to overly perceptive children. "It's true, I could do more work for the WWC. But it might mean I had less time for you guys. We would have to get a babysitter after school, or ask your Granny to help out. I don't want to have to pay for childcare that I could be doing myself."

"Right."

"And I'd miss it. Miss you guys. Lauren isn't in school yet so... maybe when she is I'll reconsider. And besides, wouldn't you miss your Mummy if I wasn't here when you got home from school?"

Vikki pursed her lips, considering. "Granny lets us have sweets," she said, as if this was all the answer needed.

Mary's phone buzzed with a text. As usual it was from Bernie.

Emergency meeting tonight, 7pm at Liz's place. B.

"Looks like you're getting your wish already," Mary said, kissing Vikki on the forehead. "Do you think your Granny will babysit for me tonight?"

"'Course she will. Although she'll probably want to watch *Strictly*. Bleugh."

"I'm going to phone her right now. Why don't you go upstairs and annoy your brothers?"

"Okay," Vikki slipped off the sofa and walked towards the stairs. "You know, I think I want to be an investigator when I grow up," she said.

"Really?" Mary felt oddly proud. "Why is that?"

"Because you get to snoop into other people's stuff."

"Don't you do that already?"

"That's why I'll be so good at it. I'm going to start with Peter's diary. He doesn't know I saw him hide it under the mattress."

Mary went to call after her and tell her not to interfere with her brother's things, but then she sat back down with her cup of tea. Sometimes it was better to wait for the inevitable fall out, rather than trying to prevent it in the first place. There was always some sort of drama going on.

On that note she wondered what was up with Bernie. They had just finished a classic case of 'find out who is shagging my husband' and Mary hadn't thought they had anything else on. But if there was something dodgy going on in Invergryff, Bernie was bound to know about it. Hopefully it would be something more interesting than the usual cheating spouses.

"Muuuuum!"

Mary put thoughts of the Wronged Women's Co-operative out of her head and wearily climbed the stairs to conduct her own investigation. This one, she suspected, wouldn't be too hard to solve.

Chapter 4: Walker

"You know what they say," Inspector Mark Saxon said, "want something done, give it to a busy person."

"But…" Sergeant Walker looked at his desktop where he had just got the hang of the latest spreadsheet. "It takes me bloody ages to do this stuff."

"That's why I've got a new assistant for you. Someone you can train up to do the tricky bits. His name is Constable Phil Higgins."

They were short-staffed, Walker thought, that was true at least. "Where's he from? I guess the help will be nice."

Saxon coughed. "He's fresh out of Tulliallan. Passed out in January."

Suddenly, it was all becoming clear. "A Probationer? That's a Constable's job to supervise. Surely someone else can…"

"Didn't you hear me, he's just passed out. Brand spanking new Constable, he just needs someone to show him the ropes."

Walker could see his every free moment of the next few weeks disappearing. "It's not normal procedure, is it? Normally they train the whole bunch of newbies at once."

"Ah, but this lad did an extra couple of months at the college, so he's out of sync with the rest. I just need you to give him a wee crash course and get him up-to-date with life outside the classroom. I've asked Constable Blake to help out too."

"And Jill Blake said yes, did she?"

The Inspector was losing patience now. "Yes she bloody well did. She understands that it isn't a request."

"All right," Walker said. "Can I ask why he finished later than the rest of his class?"

"No idea," Saxon said, but he had a slight grin on his face. He was younger than Walker despite his rank and was regarded by everyone in the office as one of those cops who knew how to play the system. "Just you make sure that he's all caught up in six weeks and we can send him off on a posting so that he's someone else's problem."

"Sure," Walker said, trying to appear happy with the situation. Not many people liked Saxon – he was a little too loud and a little too smarmy to be likeable – but he was a useful person to have on your side. And now he owed Walker a favour.

Five minutes later, Walker was in the 'break-out area' with the new arrival. The room was a particularly depressing addition to the station with uncomfortable plastic couches and weird corporate artwork on the walls. But it was a handy spot to chat outside of the office.

Constable Phil Higgins didn't look like he was enjoying himself. His shirt was a little too new and you could see where it had rubbed his neck. He was chewing his lips at any moment when he wasn't speaking. And he looked about ten years old.

"You'll like it here at Invergryff," Walker said, trying to remember how to give a pep talk. "We're a friendly bunch once you get to know us."

"Yes sir."

Don't say it, Walker told himself. They must hear it all the time. Just don't say it. "You're awfully young-looking," he heard himself say into the silence.

"Yes sir," the lad said, just about avoiding rolling his eyes. "I'm twenty-two."

"Sorry, you must get that from everyone."

"Yes sir."

Walker puffed out a breath. "Look, you don't have to do the 'sir' thing with me. I'm only a Sergeant. Save it for the ones that matter."

"Yes… sorry, I didn't catch your first name."

"It's Owen, but no one uses it. Everyone calls me Walker."

"Will I be Higgins, then?"

"No, you'll be Phil. If you're lucky and they don't find a stupid nickname for you."

Phil shuffled his feet. "Aye, they called me My Fair Lady for a while at the college."

"Did they?" Walker was impressed. "That's quite literary. I was always Shortbread. Not so clever."

"But a lot better," Phil replied.

Walker though about it. "Maybe so. Let's just stick to Phil then, eh?"

"Sure."

"Let's go and get you acquainted with the computers. I don't suppose you're any good with spreadsheets?"

"Actually, I did an HNC in computing," Phil admitted.

This time Walker's smile was genuine. "I reckon you're going to fit in just fine."

Chapter 5: Bernie

Bernie always enjoyed when they held the WWC meetings at Liz's house. Until recently, Liz had been a high-flying accountant and her husband was an optician, so she had the poshest house of the group. And it was considerably cleaner than Mary's, which was always sticky and smelled faintly of soup. The sooner that woman married her police officer boyfriend and got a nice new build on the edge of town, the better. Bernie had tried to give her that very advice, but for some reason Mary had chosen to ignore her.

They were listening to her now, however, both of them.

"Detective Inspector Macleod asked you to look into a case?" Liz asked. "I never thought he liked us very much."

"I guess he doesn't have any other choice," Mary said, topping up her fizzy wine. "If he'd had any leads he'd have solved it himself."

"He knew he needed the best," Bernie said stiffly, "so who else would he call?"

The others had no answer to that one. Mary chewed on a tortilla chip while Liz refilled Bernie's glass. Another nice thing about Liz was that she bought decent drinks. At Mary's house it was whatever she could find in the discount bin, including on one memorable occasion in June some mince pie flavour vodka. Bernie had suffered heartburn for three days after that one.

"Anyway, the copper's money is as good as anyone else's," Bernie said with a tone that said the discussion was over.

"What about our current cases?" Mary asked. "I mean, I'm just worried about the workload."

"You're all right for a bit of overtime this week though, aren't you?" Bernie asked her.

"Of course," Mary said, although she dropped her gaze to the table. Bernie hoped they weren't going to have an issue. She found managing interpersonal relationships tedious.

"It won't be an easy case, that's for sure," Bernie said, returning to the subject at hand. "I've had a quick look online. So far it's a washout. Apart from the obituary, there's no mention of Mrs Bute's death in any of the papers. Certainly nothing about any police involvement."

"I guess that's not so surprising," Mary reasoned, "if they thought she died of natural causes."

"I've only just started reading through Macleod's files. That man really should work on his handwriting. Anyway, I've managed to put the start of a report together and I've emailed you both the file. There's not much in it apart from the timeline and the details of the children."

"We don't think anyone else was involved?" Liz asked.

Bernie shook her head. "Of course, we don't really know yet. But Macleod said that the family kept to themselves. Mrs Bute's only visitors were the district nurse and a social worker – and that only seemed to be a couple of times a month – and her children, all of whom were still living at home."

"That's unusual in itself, isn't it," Mary said. "I mean, they must have been heading for thirty."

"Not the youngest. Katie Lynford. Different surname from the others due to her dad being a later partner of Mrs Bute. The family history here is a bit murky, and I'd like to know at what point Katie started living with the Butes, but that's going to be tricky. We don't even have a first name listed for her father."

"So our first job is to track down Katie Lynford, along with Joyce and Michael Bute," Mary said.

"Correct," Bernie replied. "I'm going to spend the rest of the weekend doing some intensive internet searches on them all. Mary, I want you to look into this letter that was sent to the Detective Inspector. From the so-called Mrs Volk. Macleod reckons it's a fake name as none of the neighbours has ever had that surname. So I want you to talk to all the neighbours and see if you can work out if one of them sent the letter. Start with the ones that are still there, then if that's a bust you'll have to find out who lived there when Mrs Bute was still around. Okay?"

"Okay," Mary made some notes on her phone.

"I've got another case that I think we should take on," Liz said suddenly.

"Oh?" Bernie was surprised. Liz didn't normally go looking for clients.

"It sort of fell into my lap," Liz said. She explained about the meeting in the library with Fiona Duncan.

"What a drip," Bernie said when she heard the details. "If my husband disappeared like that I'd be looking for a divorce."

"You think it's another case of the man going off with another woman?" Liz asked.

"Isn't it always?" Bernie said with a sniff. "How many times do we investigate these man-child arseholes and it comes out the same. They're too lazy and cowardly to break things off with their partner so they just run off."

"Could be," Liz said, although Bernie noticed that she wasn't giving her full agreement. "Should I start by doing a proper interview with her?"

"Yes. Get a statement out of her and then go and speak to the police. They might not tell you much, but they should at least be able to tell us if he was actually reported missing." Bernie thought of something. "If not, there's always a chance he might be buried under the patio. That's always a popular one."

"She stays in a flat," Liz replied.

"Someone else's patio then," Bernie said, not willing to let go of a good idea.

"She doesn't seem like the murdering type," Liz pointed out. "In fact, I felt sorry for her. She didn't seem like she even had a friend to talk to about it."

"Sounds like a lost cause," Bernie warned.

"I know. But she can pay. I checked her out, her parents are loaded. Her dad's into property and owns half the High Street."

This was sounding more promising. "All right then. We'll have to think about how we're going to approach this. The standard missing person stuff we normally try isn't going to be so effective after eighteen months."

Liz nodded. "I've already got a couple of ideas. Mainly social media for the moment, but I'm hoping to get into his finances if my contacts can do me a big favour there."

"Great." Bernie tapped her pen on the table. "Then I think you should work the Fiona Duncan case yourself for the moment. We can take that one a bit more slowly. Mary and I will focus on the death of Mrs Bute. Macleod could really make waves for us if we get this one right, so I want most of our energy going in that direction."

"I'm going to struggle for childcare if you want me to work tomorrow." Mary said, chewing on her thumbnail. "I mean, I've already asked my mum to come over tonight, so…"

"Just come here," Liz said. "I'll have the baby and we can send the kids upstairs. I can watch them all when you go out and talk to Mrs Bute's neighbours."

"Are you sure?"

"Of course. Just don't give them too much sugar. You remember that time that Peter had the chocolate croissant."

Mary coloured. "Don't worry, he's banned from them. I didn't even know you could block a shower drain."

The ladies did a collective shudder.

"That's decided then," Bernie said, her shoulders relaxing. She always felt better when they had a day of investigating ahead of them. "Now pour me another gin."

"Yes sir."

Chapter 6: Liz Sunday

Liz woke up on Sunday morning with just the edge of a hangover. She popped a couple of painkillers and made herself an espresso from the coffee machine that Dave had bought last month. It was shiny and chrome and had cost more than a lifetime subscription to Starbucks. But despite her disapproval of the purchase, the smell of freshly roasted coffee beans in the morning and the smooth coffee that resulted from the mechanical hissing had won her round.

"I didn't hear you come in last night," Dave said when she kissed him good morning.

"I wasn't too late, just after midnight." Liz considered making some breakfast, but settled for munching on one of the baby's sugar-free biscuits. It was just as miserable as she had imagined it would be. "Bernie has a new case for us."

"I thought you were going to get her to look at this husband who has run off," Dave said. He was in his golfing jumper which meant he was planning to get a few rounds in before work.

"We're taking that one too. But I must admit, Bernie's sounds a bit more exciting. It was the Detective Inspector himself that asked her to do it."

Dave whistled. "Are they allowed to do that?"

"Officially? Not sure. We've been listed as 'police consultants' for a while now, and Bernie says that the DI has it all worked out."

"Well done, darling," Dave said, kissing her cheek. "Issy is in the living room in her bouncer. Are you all right for me to head off?"

"Sure," Liz replied, trying not to be too offended at Dave's lack of interest in the case. He was proud of her for being a private investigator, in much the same way that he was proud of their son when he finished a computer game. Nothing phased Dave, which was one of the things she loved about him. Sometimes she just had to remind herself of that.

Sean came into the room, hair sticking up and eyes bleary from sleep. She pulled him into a hug that he pretended not to like. He was twelve, at that awkward age when you were half-kid, half-adult, but mostly just made of legs.

"You need some new PJs," Liz said, noting that they were rising above his ankles.

"Yeah, guess so." Sean yawned wide like a cat. "I've got that project to do for geology. Can you help me with the rivers?"

He had decided to do Nigeria for his country project, looking at flood plains. His grandmother had been pleased and given him a fiver for it, which might have been his plan all along. Liz had promised to help with the model but hadn't had a chance yet.

"Ah, sorry, I've got Mary coming around with her kids later. We're going to do some online research on some missing people. One case with a husband who has absconded and another with an entire family that have disappeared."

Sean's head drooped.

"I've probably got an hour before then, if you'd like me to take a look?" Liz backtracked quickly. "I could –"

Just at that moment a loud wail started in the living room.

"Forget about it," Sean muttered and stomped off upstairs.

Liz wanted to go after him, but Isioma's cries were becoming insistent. When she went into the living room, she discovered a full nappy and a very unhappy face. Once she had changed her, Bernie rang with another list of instructions and her mother phoned to firm up childcare arrangements for the week. A half-hour had gone past before she could even think about Sean upstairs in his room.

"Crap," Liz said, jiggling the baby on her hip and making another coffee. When Issy had been born, she and Dave had made an effort to ensure that Sean didn't feel left out. But in reality, it was impossible to avoid. He had gone from an only child to a reluctant older brother. If only there was a better way to get him involved, other than changing nappies which he had so far declined to do.

Still with the baby next to her, Liz turned on her laptop and did some reasonably successful multitasking with a baby bottle and a notepad. The first thing she wanted to do was make up a timeline of the missing man. She had scheduled an interview with Fiona for eight o'clock that evening, but before she went

Liz wanted to know as much as possible about the family. And the best place to do that sort of snooping was social media.

Fiona didn't seem to have an account on any of the main social media channels, but her mother did and it didn't take long for Liz to find it. Christine Robinson liked to post anything and everything online. Mostly pictures of herself drinking expensive cocktails in the Mediterranean. If her online presence was to be believed, she was a jet-setting early retiree, 'loving life' and certainly enjoying spending her money. There were several posts of handbags that made Liz more than a little jealous, especially considering that she hadn't bought a designer bag since giving up her well-paid job last year. Still, happiness was better than being rich, she reasoned, and it was possible to be happy without fancy handbags. Probably.

"Can I get a snack," Sean asked, poking his head around the door.

"Sure," Liz said. "There's fruit in the bowl or you can grab a sandwich." She typed in Fiona Duncan's name into the search engine again, but was still struggling to find her online. Then she saw a website with a capital P and a lightning bolt, listing a profile for Fifi Duncan.

When Liz went to click on the link, she hit a security screen asking for a password.

"Damn," she said.

"What is it?" Sean asked, coming over to her shoulder.

"Have you seen this site before? One of my clients is on it, but I don't know what it is."

Sean looked at the link. "'Course, it's called Plnz. Like plans, you know?"

Liz had never felt so old. "All right, so it's just another social media thing, right?"

"I guess. It's for people that don't like videos or images. Sort of an old-school twitter before it went crazy."

"I see. But you're not on this, right? Because I've banned all social media until you're twenty-five, right?"

Sean gave her his most angelic face. "Of course, mum. But some of the guys at school have it."

Liz spun her laptop around. "Okay, then I want you to set up a profile on it."

"For real?"

"Yes. But not in your name. Do it in a fake one, please, I'll give you the name." Liz brought up her spreadsheet of false identities.

"Gogo Pinyatta?" Sean said, reading over her shoulder.

"That was for the sort of case I can only tell you about when you hit eighteen," Liz said. "Here's one we can use, Maggie Grant." Maggie was one of her favourite identities, seeing as she had her own website and social media profiles. Maggie loved long walks, cream teas and Bichon Frises. Her social media was full of stock images of the hairy little dogs and Liz had spent many happy hours online finding the appropriate photos.

Maggie Grant set up a profile on Plnz, with Sean's help and soon Liz was able to access Fiona Duncan's profile. There were minimal pictures and a lot of short posts, mainly about whatever political cause was in the news at the time. Fiona appeared to see no contradiction in supporting veganism, local farmers, socialism, anti-capitalism, support for small businesses, intervention in China, non-intervention in Syria and so on. Every cause you could think of was mentioned, and often both sides. Still, she seemed harmless enough. Liz had just scrolled back to the point in time when Fiona's husband went missing when the doorbell rang.

Mary's kids entered in their usual whirlwind. Liz sent them into the dining room where she had prepared an arrangement of craft and board games to keep them busy.

"Do you need more help, mum, or can I show Peter my new game?" Sean asked with pleading eyes.

"Off you go," Liz said.

"Don't be uploading any racist memes now," Sean called with a grin as he left the room.

"I'll try not to," Liz said. In answer to Mary's raised eyebrow, she explained how Sean had helped her set up an account on Plnzs. Then she added: "You don't have to say anything. I know I shouldn't be letting him help."

Mary held out her hands, palms upwards. "I am not one to judge. Believe me. Just this week I let Peter do the shopping by himself and he bought everything on the list then added a packet of Mentos and some cheap cola. Unfortunately, I didn't check the receipt until he had already started his 'experiment'."

"Oh god," Liz said, putting her hands over her eyes.

"Yeah. He set it off under Walker's car, hoping the force would move it or something, I don't know. What I do know is that it's quite expensive to get cola foam out of every orifice of what was a new Peugeot."

When Liz had stopped laughing, she had forgotten what they were talking about.

"You were worried about Sean helping you with work," Mary reminded her.

"Maybe I should tell him to stop," Liz said. "It's not exactly child-appropriate, is it?"

Mary picked some toast crumbs off the bottom of her trousers. "I don't know, maybe it's a way you two can spend time together. It can't be easy for him now that he's sharing attention with the baby."

"True. How do you manage it?"

"Oh, a lot of caffeine for me and a lot of bickering for them. And an anger tent where they can go and cool off in the garden. I guess it all works out in the end. There are all speaking to me, at any rate."

Chapter 7: Mary

Mary was usually a tea drinker, but she was very much enjoying the fancy cappuccino that Liz had made from her new coffee machine. Especially once she had added three sugars to it.

"Do you think the kids are all right," she asked, licking the foam from her lips. "I haven't heard much from them."

"They're probably all on screens," Liz replied. Isioma had gone down for her nap and the house was strangely quiet. "They'll come and get us when they want some lunch."

"What do you reckon about Macleod asking Bernie to look at this cold case," Mary asked. "I mean, she was practically buzzing with pride."

"It's good news, and not just for Bernie. If we want the WWC to be a legitimate business going forward, we need to start branching out into corporate services."

Mary blinked. "Sorry, what?"

"Oh, I just mean that missing cats and even the occasional murder aren't going to pay the bills for the three of us, especially when I'm back at work full time. If we can start working for big companies – whether that's public sector like the police, or the private sector – then we might just have a long-term future."

Business lingo was not Mary's strong point, but she thought

she was following along. "Do you think if we don't do this then our future will be in doubt?"

"Of course. And Bernie knows that too. At the end of the day, we all need our salaries paid, one way or the other."

"I just had a chat with Vikki about going full time," Mary said.

"Bernie's been asking you for months, hasn't she?"

"Yeah, but I just don't know about the childcare part. I mean, I don't want my mum having to do more than she already does. It's bad enough trying to get a date night with Walker once a month."

"Well, why don't we share a childminder? You know, in a few months when Issy turns one, we could look at hiring someone together. That would make it a lot more affordable."

"Thanks, we could definitely consider it," Mary replied. She knew that Liz was doing her a kindness. With her fancy eye doctor husband, Liz didn't have the same financial worries and could easily have afforded her own childminder. And yet, something was holding Mary back. "Let's talk about it closer to the time."

Liz led them through to the living room where Mary set up station in the bay window, curling up on a large armchair and balancing her laptop on her knee.

"I'm going to take a look through all Fiona's Duncan's posts around the time her husband disappeared," Liz said, opening up her own computer. "I want to be fully armed when I go to interview her."

"Do you think she was telling you the truth? I mean, that she had no idea he was going to run off."

"Probably not. No one wants to admit that their marriage is in crisis, do they?"

Mary shuddered. "God no. Mine was a mess for years before I finally left. And now we're both much happier. Matt is even talking about getting married again."

"To the wonderful Stephanie?"

"Yes. And as new wives go, she wouldn't be the worst. The kids adore her. I just wish she was a bit less... well, herself, you know? She's a lot to live up to."

"Oh come on, your kids love you to bits," Liz said.

"They do, but I have to be the grumpy parent all the time. I'm the one shouting at them to do their homework and wash their hair properly. But with Stephanie it's all let's make ceramic models of ourselves and family photoshoots in the woods and sustainable camping. I tried to take them camping once and Vikki saw a dragonfly, freaked out and wouldn't go outside for a week. Stephanie takes them all glamping in Perthshire and they turn into woodland nymphs."

Liz was staring at her.

"Sorry, was that a bit ranty?"

"A little."

"I really want to like her. I don't want to be the jealous ex-wife. And I'm genuinely not jealous of her having to put up with Matt. But I guess I do feel like a little green-eyed monster when she's hanging out with the kids."

"Perfectly natural," Liz replied.

Mary decided it was time to move on from this thorny subject. She looked at the notes she had taken about the day's research.

"Bernie wants me to start by looking into the children of Mrs Bute, so I'm going to do some searching online." For a few minutes there was silence in the room as Liz and Mary both tapped away at their keyboards.

From what Bernie had told her, Mrs Bute's daughter, son and stepdaughter had disappeared a week after their mother's funeral. Their files on them were correspondingly brief.

Mr Michael Bute had been twenty-seven in 2012, so he would be thirty-seven or eight by now. Detective Inspector Macleod's notes listed his profession as 'mechanic', but whether that meant he worked in a garage or somewhere else, Mary couldn't tell. There was no job listed for his sister, Joyce, who would be around thirty-five now. Neither were listed as having a partner or children.

There were even less details for the younger girl, Katie. Macleod had managed to find a grainy picture of her which looked like it had been cut out from a class photo at school. It wasn't much help. Big, watery eyes that might have been blue or green. Lank dirty blond hair that hung down her face.

Mary felt a pang of empathy for the girl. Being a certified geek in high school had meant that Mary had often wanted to disappear. She couldn't help but feel that Katie felt the same way. Macleod hadn't said the word abuse, but the way he had called the social work in suggested that he was worried about something going on in that family. What was that frightened little face hiding?

Even though Bernie had already tried, Mary started with a simple search of the name 'Katie Lynford'. Nothing much came up and anything that did appear in that name was other people with variations of Katherine Lynford, mostly in America.

The first thing to do was to request a copy of the birth certificate. That, thankfully, was easy enough to do through the official Scotland's People website. Unfortunately, even with fast track postage it would take a day or two to arrive. All she could see from the online entry was that Katherine Lynford had been born in the district of Lanarkshire in 1992. Mary was dying to know what had happened to Katie's birth mother and her father, but she would have to wait until the certificate arrived before she could even find out their names.

And what about Mrs Bute's husband, presumably called Mr Bute? Macleod's file hadn't mentioned him at all, so perhaps he was dead. Without a first name, any searches weren't likely to find anything. Instead, Mary turned her focus on Joyce and Michael.

It was quickly becoming apparent that searching Scottish people named 'Bute' on general search engines was a nightmare due to the name being the same as the island. Mary quickly turned to the social media sites instead.

"Can you check on Pulanzee to see if Michael and Joyce Bute are on there?" Mary asked.

"It's pronounced Planz, apparently," Liz replied. She typed for a moment, then shook her head. "Sorry, no sign. Nothing's coming up for Katie Lynford either."

Mary crossed her arms. "I really think it's selfish of people to stay off social media. How are we meant to snoop into their private lives if it's not online?"

"We'll just have to talk to them, like in the olden days," Liz smiled. "Speaking of which I've got to head off and get over to Fiona Duncan's house. You'll be all right with all the kids until I get back."

"Oh yeah, I'm used to the madness."

"If Issy wakes up, there's an expressed bottle in the fridge."

Mary was secretly hoping the baby would wake up. She wasn't broody anymore – that period of her life was well past, thank goodness – but other people's babies were still a joy. The more cuddles she could get before one of the more demanding children needed her, the better.

Once Liz had left, Mary checked on the bigger children – no one was sporting any new bruises and there had been minimal damage to furniture, so far it was a successful playdate – and considered making herself a fancy coffee. She looked at the range of knobs and dials on the big chrome machine and reached for the kettle instead. Better safe than sorry.

Just as she was squishing the tea bag against the mug to get every last drop of caffeine out, her phone rang.

"Hello my sexy little Terminator."

"I'd rather you didn't call me that," Walker said. "As I think I have already mentioned."

Mary giggled. "All right. It's just I was watching T2 last night and that bit when he's frowning at people and all cheekbones in his cop uniform. It just reminded me of you."

"That murderous robot reminded you of me?"

"Yeah."

"I've got some info about a cold case for Bernie, but she's not answering her phone."

Mary checked her watch. "Ah, it's her Nordic walking class right now."

"Nordic what? Never mind. Actually, are you free? I'd much rather spend an hour with you than her anyhow."

"Sure. I'm at Liz's, but you can pop over."

There was the sound of a mumbled conversation. "All right. I've just got someone to drop off, then I'll head on over."

"Great."

Chapter 8: Walker

After he had dropped off Phil Higgins, Walker drove up to Liz's house and made sure to park so that he didn't block the garage. Liz's husband, Dave, had a couple of nice cars, including a Boxster that Walker was hoping to get a ride in at some point. So far his hints had not reached the man, but there was still time.

Mary opened the door when he rang and Walker felt a smile tug at his lips. It was weird. Her outfit was the opposite of what should be attractive: ripped jeans that were probably last fashionable when Justin Timberlake wore them, hair pulled into two messy pigtails secured with her daughter's butterfly clips and an oversized hoodie with Batgirl on the front. Or Mrs Spiderman, or something. It was hard to keep up. On anyone else it would have looked ridiculous. But on Mary Plunkett it was certifiably adorable. Walker had never been able to work out why. It was probably best not to question it.

"Everything okay?"

Mary pulled a stray strand of hair from her face. "Yes. Peter managed to put a whole carrot into the coffee roaster, but I've managed to get it all out. You can hardly smell it now."

That last remark was patently untrue, but Liz's kitchen did at least look relatively tidy.

"How are the kids?"

"Not too bad. Liz set up a whole arcade for them in the dining room. I'm just giving little Issy some mush for lunch."

Walker took note of the chubby armed creature in the high chair. She was waving a spoon of orange puree around and he made sure to stand on the other side of the kitchen so as to be out of range. Going out with Mary meant he had to become comfortable with kids fairly quickly, but babies still terrified him. You never knew what they were going to do next.

"Blub," Issy said, spitting up onto her chin.

"Isn't she precious," Mary said, in a blatant disregard of the evidence.

"Hmmn," Walker went over to the coffee machine. It looked like it belonged on one of those terrible space shows Mary was always trying to get him to watch. "This must have cost a fortune."

"I guess so," Mary said. "They can afford it though, can't they? Matt used to love a gadget when we had the big house in Aberdeen, but even he didn't have anything this swish. Besides, Stephanie's got him on the decaf now."

"How are Matt and Stephanie," Walker said, doing his best to seem interested. In fact, he found Mary's ex-husband a bit of a puzzle. He managed to be both dull and irritating in equal measures, and the one time they had all gone out together – for the sake of the children – he had ended up in a long, tedious discussion about football, which neither of them were particularly interested in but was the only neutral topic they could find. The idea that Mary, his Mary, had spent more than a decade with this person was baffling.

"They are fine," Mary said, unaware that he was still musing over her ex. "Still talking about a wedding, even though the divorce won't be through for months. The kids are happy about being bridesmaids and groomsmen, although Johnny has decided he's going to be the wedding photographer, so God help them on that one."

"You don't find it weird?" Walker asked. "You know, talking about Matt's new wedding?"

Mary laughed. "What, given that I was one of the main characters in the last one? I left him, remember. I'm not going to be crying in the aisle."

"Of course not," Walker said, trying to make light of it. How had he gone down this road anyway?"

"Is something the matter?" Mary asked.

"No. Not really. Sorry, I'm just fed up because of work. They've lumped this new probationer on me."

"I didn't think you were doing that right now. Don't the new recruits normally turn up at the start of the year?"

"I'm not supposed to be. But he passed out later than the rest of his year at the college. There's a story there, I'm sure of it, but no one seems to know what. All I know is that I've got to babysit him as well as do all my work."

"Maybe you just need to bond with him a bit," Mary suggested.

"He's barely out of his teens. We've got nothing in common. I don't even know what people in their twenties get up to in 2024."

"Hang on." Mary opened the door to the dining room. "Vikki, what are twenty year olds into these days?"

"Drill music and protein shakes," a small voice shouted back.

"See," she smiled. "Easy peasy."

"I'll make a note," Walker said. "Anyway, just before I left the station I got a request through from Bernie. She wanted some info on a cold case of Macleod's."

Mary nodded. "That's right. Macleod has asked the WWC to look into it." There was a definite note of pride in her voice, and Walker couldn't blame her. Even he had considered the WWC to be barely more than a joke when he had first met them. And here they were, officially recognised consultants to the police.

He reached into his laptop bag and brought out the files. "I'm not really meant to print these out, but Bernie was insistent. She doesn't get any easier, does she?"

"Nope," Mary said, grabbing the stack of paper. "That's what makes her so brilliant. What am I looking at here?"

"Anything from the police databases on Mrs Bute and her relations. There's not much there, I'm sorry to say. Far too law-abiding to make our jobs easier. There were no hits at all on Joyce Bute or Katie Lynford. And just one for Michael Bute."

"Ooh, let's have a look at that," Mary said, flicking through the papers. "Is it this one? It just looks like a traffic offense. Broken headlight eight years ago, given a caution for it. Wasn't there anything else?"

"Not really. There's more stuff about the family from years ago. Apparently Mrs Bute's partner, Joe Lynford, had a bit of a record. I didn't have a chance to go through it, but you might find something there that the officers missed at the time."

"Like evidence for a murder?"

Walker shrugged. "If Macleod thinks there was something unnatural about Mrs Bute's death, then I'd be hard-pressed to disagree with him. He's the best DI I've worked with. But proving it will be another matter."

Chapter 9: Bernie

Nordic walking was turning out to be a total farce. When Bernie had first discovered it, she had watched videos of people marching around in the Winter Olympics and had thought it would be right up her street.

Unfortunately, she hadn't considered the age range of people who liked walking in the park on a Sunday afternoon. She was the youngest there by a good couple of decades, and what she had imagined would be a sprint across challenging terrain turned out to be a gentle dawdle around the duck pond.

"You're really a private investigator?" A nasal voice said in Bernie's ear. "I thought that was only on the telly."

"We're a lot better than the ones you see on Sunday night drama," Bernie snapped at the stringy-limbed man beside her. "And probably a lot cheaper."

"My friend's cat went missing last week and –"

"But we don't do missing cats," Bernie said quickly. "Cats are autonomous beings and if they decide to move on that's no one's business but their own."

The man's mouth dropped open and Bernie used his moment of shock to power on ahead so that she could cross the finish line first.

"Well done," an elderly woman in a rain mac said. "Not that

it's a race, of course."

"It's always a race." Bernie muttered as she flung her borrowed poles onto the ground. Honestly, apart from some of the fitness classes at the gym where she was working with men who ate raw eggs in the same way Mary Plunkett ate chocolate eclairs, Bernie was starting to give up on Invergryff's attempts at exercise sessions. Maybe she should start up her own class. She could call it 'No Wimps Allowed'. It had a nice ring to it.

After she got home and took a quick shower, she decided to spend some time on Macleod's cold case. She had already lined up Mary to go and interview the neighbours, but Bernie had a secret weapon that she wanted to use first.

It hadn't taken her long to find out who the social worker was that had worked with the Bute family. She knew that Mrs Bute's parenting had already been flagged up to care providers by Macleod, and from there it was just a case of working out who had been referred to her.

Bernie's sister Laura had come through in the end. Laura was one of her least favourite siblings, given her interest in reality TV shows and the tendency to spend all her time shopping. But she had worked in child services for years and had a memory for names that often came in handy. It took a promise of a shopping trip and a contribution towards a new leather handbag before Laura told Bernie about Emily Cookes.

Cookes was the head social worker that had covered that area of Invergryff at the time of Mrs Bute's death. Once Bernie knew the name it was easy enough to get the woman's number and arrange a meeting that evening.

Retired witnesses were always Bernie's favourite kinds, mainly because they adhered less strictly to the whole 'client confidentiality' thing. But when she arrived at Mrs Emily Cookes's house, it was clear that the problem would be getting the woman to stop talking, not worrying about the woman keeping her mouth shut.

"I've been retired for eight years now, did my thirty years for the council before then. You wouldn't believe some of the things I've seen."

"I bet I would," Bernie said happily. For a witness this chatty she had even been persuaded to take a bourbon biscuit, which was now coating her mouth with an unpleasant gritty sweetness.

"I started out on the South East side of the town in the eighties. Quite a nice little patch, mainly the posh houses over on Southwold Avenue, you know? Then after three years they moved me to the South West, that new estate past the supermarket. You know it?"

Bernie nodded.

"Well, that was a bit of a rude awakening, I can tell you. Lots of immigrants – not that I've got anything against that, my nephew's girlfriend is Spanish, you see – and lots of women with kids from half a dozen different partners. Well!" The woman was rendered momentarily speechless by the depths of Invergryff's depravity.

Bernie took a deep mouthful of tea to get rid of the biscuit remnants, then realised that the milk was on the turn. She forced herself to swallow. "And that's where Mrs Bute lived?"

Mrs Cookes leaned forward. "You understand that I can't tell you anything private about them? I mean, I couldn't do anything that would get anyone in trouble."

"This is a murder inquiry," Bernie said sternly. She had seen Inspector Frost say this on one of the reruns on the telly the other day.

"Murder? But I thought she died naturally?"

"So did the police at the time," Bernie said.

The older lady shuffled in her seat. "Well, I would want to help see justice done like anyone else. I protested the Iraq war, you know."

"Good for you," Bernie replied. "Now, if we could get back to Mrs Bute?"

"I was first involved with the husband, you see. Leonard Bute. That was when he got ill."

Bernie made sure her phone was set to record. So far, they hadn't even managed to find out Mrs Bute's late husband's name. Mrs Cookes was already proving herself worth the refined sugar consumption.

"Her husband was sick?"

"Yes. This was years ago. I want to say around 1990.

Leonard Bute was on our list because the council had made some adaptations to their house, so we had to do a check to make sure they weren't faking it. You wouldn't believe what people will do to get some free stuff."

"But Leonard wasn't faking it?"

"Oh no. He had one of those lung things, CPD I think, or something similar. Had to have oxygen in the house. But I only visited once. Mrs Bute did all of his care. She was devoted to him."

Mrs Cookes looked out the window as she spoke, which made Bernie's ears prick up.

"Devoted?"

"Yeah. She couldn't do enough for him."

"But there was something funny about that, was there?" Bernie prompted.

Mrs Cookes sighed. "It was the children. They were young then, maybe under ten. And all the time that Mrs Bute fussed over her husband she never mentioned them once. Never even looked at them. I got the feeling they were left to fend for themselves."

"You were worried about neglect?"

"I wouldn't go as far as that. We have a threshold that needs to be met before we apply those sorts of terms. The children were clean and healthy. But there was just a… a vibe of something not quite right. So over the years I kept an eye on them, or I tried to."

"Tell me the rest," Bernie said.

The woman let out another sigh. Bernie was beginning to find it irritating. Like speaking to a mechanical fan.

"Michael got in a bit of trouble at school when he hit his teens. It was referred to the Children's Panel, and we made a few follow-up visits. He was fighting, now that's not unusual for boys, but there was the suggestion of some unsavoury behaviour towards the girls as well. But no one made any formal statements, so again it just went away."

"Doesn't sound like people wanted to do anything about it," Bernie said.

"You have no idea what it was like," Mrs Cookes said, her back straightening. "We had families where the whole lot of them were on drugs, kids that never knew where they'd be sleeping, mothers that drank all through their pregnancies… in comparison, the Butes were like Little House on the Prairie."

"So they slipped through the gaps?"

The woman shrugged but didn't say anything else.

"There was another partner after her husband, wasn't there? A Mr Lynford?"

"I believe so. The family were off our books by then. It wasn't until much later that we paid them a visit. A few years before Mrs Bute passed away, in fact."

"Oh yes?"

Once again, Mrs Cookes looked uncomfortable. "It was the school that had asked for a home visit. They were worried about a young girl who was living with the Butes. She had missed quite a lot of school and they wanted some support from us to find out why."

"This would be Katie Lynford."

"Yes. A slip of a thing. Shy as you like. I did the meeting myself. Mrs Bute didn't seem to be any better than she had a decade before, barely interested in what her children were doing. But Michael and Joyce were grown up by now and they showed me around. Food in the fridge, the girl's room was clean and tidy. I didn't spot any signs of abuse or neglect. In fact, it was rather the opposite."

"Really?"

"Yes. The sister, Joyce. She was reading the child a storybook when I came in. I got the sense that she cared for that kid like it was her own, rather than a sister. They maybe weren't the happiest family I've ever met, but they weren't the worst either. Not by a long way."

"What if one of them killed their mother? That might make them the worst."

Mrs Cookes didn't look too impressed. "Unless you can prove it, then I won't believe it. Many people hate their parents, more than you would think. But hardly any of them commit murder."

Bernie pulled on her coat. "Maybe they just don't get caught."

Chapter 10: Liz

Fiona Duncan took forever to answer her door. She lived in a small flat overlooking the Abbey in the centre of Invergryff. This was the first anomaly that Liz had noted. A few phone calls that morning to some friends in the business community had confirmed that Fiona's parents were officially loaded. So what was their daughter doing in this cramped little place, not to mention their only grandchild?

"Marco's sleeping," Fiona said when she showed Liz into the living room. The skinny woman had her arms folded and could not have looked more defensive. Liz was starting to get a bad feeling about the whole thing, but she sat down on the sofa and took out her notepad anyway.

"I've been doing some research on Lucas going missing. I haven't managed to get the police to talk to me about the missing person report."

Fiona sat down and clasped her hands on her knees. "They weren't interested. They said because he had taken his wallet and his passport and everything that he wasn't in any danger. That he was 'voluntarily absent', whatever that means."

"Why don't you start from... well, from the start."

"It was a Friday night and we'd had a horrible row. We didn't fight much, you know, but sometimes... well, it's hard bringing up a kid, isn't it? He went to sleep on the sofa and that's why I didn't realise that he was gone until Marco woke up the next morning at around seven."

"And you said that he took his passport and his wallet?"

Fiona nodded. "I didn't realise that at first. We kept stuff like that in the bedside table. But when he didn't come home that night I called the police and they said to see if he'd taken anything. That's when I realised he'd taken a holdall with a few bits, some clothes and his passport."

This wasn't sounding promising. "Do you think he planned to go abroad?"

"Maybe. I guess you would have to stop the investigation then, wouldn't you?"

"Not necessarily. We can check out expat communities if he's gone to somewhere like Spain or France. Further afield might be a bit tougher."

"There's not much hope then," Fiona said, picking at a worn section on the arm of the sofa.

"But you want us to keep looking, don't you?" Liz asked.

Fiona shrugged. "Maybe it's not the right time."

"You seemed keen the other day?" Liz reminded her. She mentally added: at least I've already taken a deposit.

The younger woman sniffed. "I told my dad I had called you in."

Ah, there it was. "He didn't approve?"

Fiona shrugged again. "Doesn't matter what he thinks, does it? But for some stupid reason he told Mum, and she went off on one. Started saying how I was going to drag everything up again and just cause trouble. She never liked Lucas anyway."

"Didn't she?"

"No. Lucas was a bit... wild, when we first got together, I mean. And he wasn't exactly golf club material, you know? But since Marco was born he'd been a lot better. He was working as a gardener, paying towards the bills, all the crap that Mum and Dad wanted him to do. But they still couldn't bear to be in the same room as him."

"And Marco?"

"They don't give a crap about him either. Oh, they'll buy him some fancy toy for Christmas, or put money into his savings account. But they never make the effort to come and visit. He barely recognises them."

Liz was starting to feel genuine sympathy for the woman. It was one thing to disapprove of your daughter's partner, but quite another to ignore your own grandson. Mr and Mrs Robinson did not seem like good people. Liz mentally added them to her list of suspects. Suspects for what, she wasn't too sure, but she definitely wanted them on there.

"What did your parents say when Lucas left?"

"Good riddance, basically. They said he'd probably gone abroad or something. Or found someone else. And then when he sent the email that was it. Mum said that he'd proved himself to be the deadbeat dad she always thought he was."

"Email?"

Fiona's neck reddened. "I wasn't sure whether or not to show you it. It doesn't exactly make him look good."

"If it's relevant to the case then you should show me it," Liz said sternly.

"All right," Fiona said, pulling out her phone. She scrolled through for a second, then handed it over so that Liz could read it.

Sorry about everything. I've been a right tosser. Look after Marco for me.

Not much of a message for someone to disappear off the face of the earth, Liz thought. A horrible thought struck her: it could be just the sort of thing someone would write for a suicide note.

"When did he send this?"

"A couple of days after he disappeared. And that's the last I heard from him. Over a year ago. He's never phoned or emailed, or asked about his son…" Fiona rubbed at her eyes, streaking mascara onto her cheek.

"Did he suffer with depression at all?" Liz asked.

"Not really. He was more… almost hyper, you know? Always up to something. Get rich schemes, that sort of stuff. He was, well, maybe not that bright. But I loved him. And Marco loved him. And I just really want him back so I can slap his stupid face."

The tears started for real by then. Liz reached into her bag and brought out some tissues. Bernie had made them all take an emergency kit with them on WWC calls and that included tissues, packs of raisins to keep up the blood sugar and a rape alarm. Just in case.

"I'll call you when I find something," Liz said as she left the flat. But she wasn't feeling overly hopeful. If she'd known about the passport and the email Lucas had sent, she probably wouldn't even have taken the case in the first place. But they were committed now so she would have to make the best of it.

When Liz got home she found Isioma in her bouncer and Mary napping on the sofa next to her. Liz let out a strategic cough.

"Sorry," Mary said, rubbing her eyes, "it's just that Lauren was up last night and… oh, god, was I drooling?"

"No," Liz lied. "Don't worry about it. Are you still okay to go and do some interviews?"

"Of course," Mary replied. "I'm going to see if I can get anything out of Mrs Bute's neighbours. Bernie reckons it'll be a bust, but it's got to be worth a try. Maybe one of them heard a fight or something."

"Sure," Liz said, not feeling quite so hopeful. Most people couldn't remember what happened to them last week, let alone a decade ago.

Mary gathered her handbag together.

"Do I smell carrots?" Liz said, sniffing the air.

"Don't think so," Mary said a little too quickly. "Right, you're sure you're okay to watch the others while I pop over to do some door-knocking?"

"Of course," Liz replied. She had already formulated a secret babysitting plan that mainly involved ordering pizza. You were always a hero to kids if you provided zero home cooking and lots of empty calories. She might even add some ice-cream.

Just after Mary left, Sean came down the stairs with his notebook computer balanced on one hand.

"Can I show you something?"

"Sure," Liz said, popping Isioma down on the floor so that she could pull herself up on the sofa. Mary's kids were watching Jurassic Park in the living room, which Liz had suggested might not be appropriate before the kids explained they watched it every Sunday, even the four year old.

"I've been doing some research on that guy that's gone missing. That Fiona Duncan's boyfriend, Lucas."

Liz took in a deep breath. "What do you mean, research?"

"Online snooping. You know, like you taught me."

"You shouldn't be doing that without me there. Especially on those social media sites."

Sean's bottom lip stuck out. "You do it."

"And I am an adult, not to mention a professional," Liz said, hating that she sounded like her mother. "Besides, these sorts of cases, it's not like a missing cat, they could be dangerous."

"Bernie said you weren't doing cats anymore."

"Yes, well, that's beside the point." Liz tried to stay calm. The thing was, she'd grown up with Nigerian parents, and part of her felt like the natural mode of parenting was to whoop ass as much as possible. But she had also learned liberal parenting from middle-class Scotland where children were allowed to speak their mind and generally do whatever the hell they liked. Somehow, as she swung between these two extremes her son had managed to grow up without turning into a psychopath, so she figured children were a lot more resilient than most people thought.

"Why don't you show me what you found out," she said finally. "Then I'll decide whether or not to be mad at you." Parenting sorted, she got Sean to hand over the laptop.

"All right, so I haven't found your missing guy. But I did find his sister. And she's a right weirdo."

"We try not to use words like 'weirdo', remember?" Liz said, looking over his shoulder.

"But look, mum, she's got pictures of unicorns all over her socials."

"Okay, that isn't a good sign. But still, try and avoid 'weirdo', will you? I mean, some of our best friends are more than a little weird."

"You're talking about Mary Plunkett, aren't you?"

Liz coughed. "Not necessarily."

"Peter says that she watches *Titanic* once a month and spends the whole time shouting at some woman to 'move over and let Leo live!'"

"Eccentric, not weird. There's a difference. Tell me about this sister, will you?"

"Her username on the social stuff is Roro Duncan. And as I said, most of the posts that are public are those silly sayings like 'if life hands you lemons' and pictures of unicorns. Gross, right?"

"Right. What else did you find?"

"I was looking for family pics. But the thing is, there's only one picture of her and her brother. It was posted like eight years ago too, so it doesn't look like they were close."

Liz looked at the picture in question. It showed Lucas Duncan and the sister whose real name seemed to be Roxanne, judging by the comments from other people below the picture. They were sat in a restaurant with a group of people and some 40th birthday balloons.

"Did you find any mention of Marco on there?"

"Marco? Who's that?"

"Lucas's son. That would make him her nephew."

"No, none at all. I mean, they could be private I guess, but

69

seeing as she lets all the rest of her stuff be marked public, I wouldn't think so."

"All right, I guess you did a good job. I still don't want you on social media though, not when I'm not around to supervise it."

"Everyone else does it," Sean said.

"If everyone else jumped... Hang on, I'm not falling into this trap. Look, at some point when you're older I'll be happy for you to post whatever the hell you like online. But just now I'd rather you didn't ruin your life before it even gets started."

"Mu-um," Sean said with a classic teen eye-roll.

"Off you go. Why don't you show Peter your new keyboard? And don't forget the headphones."

Her son had so far displayed little musical talent, and that suited Liz just fine. Sean's teacher had mentioned the recorder at one point, but Liz had once visited Mary's house during a violin session and after that she had banned all musical instruments. Well, except for ones like keyboards that could be played with headphones.

"Love you mum," Sean said as he rushed out of the door.

"Love you too," she said in the second before the baby started to cry.

Chapter 11: Mary

The street where Mrs Bute used to live was typical of Invergryff, or in fact any small town in central Scotland. It had been built mainly post-war with a few newer buildings dotted around. Pebbledash was the finish of choice, much like the stuff Mary had had hacked off her own house as soon as she'd moved in.

The first address for Mary to try was Mrs Bute's own house. She knocked on the door and was greeted by a man in his fifties. When Mary explained that she wanted to find out about the former occupier the man explained that the house had been bought and sold three times since then and he had never even heard of the woman.

"You might want to try Ronnie Goldberg over there," he said, pointing at the house diagonally opposite. "She's about a thousand years old so she might remember them."

Pleased with this information, Mary hurried over to the other neighbour. She knocked on the door, but there was no reply.

"She probably thinks you're the Jehovah's," a voice said from behind her. The new resident of Mrs Bute's house had followed her across the road. "I'll get her for you."

He preceded to thump on the glass on the living room window. Mary felt her shoulders rise into cringe position. Luckily, when Ronnie finally answered the door she didn't seem to mind.

"It's yourself is it John? Let me guess, you've blocked up that sink again and you want to borrow my plunger."

The woman had the weirdest accent Mary had ever heard. It was half Irish, half New York Jewish. The sort of accent that seemed to give you a warm hug all on its own.

"I've brought you a visitor, Ronnie. She wants to know about someone that lived in my house before I got here."

"The Stuarts?"

"No, before that. What was the name?"

"Mrs Bute," Mary replied. Did she imagine it or did Ronnie's wrinkled smile flicker for a second?

"Ah, so it is. You better come in then."

For a moment Mary thought that her new friend was going to follow them in, but she made sure to thank him for his help and close the door before he could join them.

"I don't suppose you would like a scone, would you? I've got the grandchildren coming around after school tomorrow and I always bake too many. Scones were the first Scottish recipe I managed to master when we moved over here from the US."

Maybe it wouldn't be so bad to do this full time, Mary thought as Ronnie brought her a huge scone topped with a scoop of homemade raspberry jam on each fluffy half.

"Uff ooh know if ell?" Mary asked.

"Sorry dear?" Ronnie had settled down on the sofa with a tea and a small cat that was tremendously overweight.

Mary swallowed. "I mean to say, did you know them well? Mrs Bute and her family?"

"Well, they kept to themselves. I saw the husband a few times before he got ill. He was a bit of a charmer. Or liked to think he was. One of those sort of shallow men, you understand? Expected a lot from his family without doing much in return."

This was turning out to be a great interview, Mary thought. There was nothing better than a gossipy neighbour.

"This would be Leonard Bute. He passed away when the children were still young, didn't he?"

"Yes. I'm not sure from what exactly. He started walking with a cane, then he stopped going out of the house. It was then that Mrs Bute started to disappear as well."

"Disappear?"

Ronnie shrugged. "She spent all her time looking after him. So when he was sick the whole lot of them barely left the house. Even those two odd little kids. They never went and played outside with the others. Mind you, they never egged anyone's front doors either, so maybe there was something to be said for it."

She coughed a little then sipped her tea. The elderly cat yawned fish breath across the room.

"But now that I think about it, a bit of rebellion might have done them good. I always thought... well, I thought there was something wrong in that family. They were frightened of someone. And I guessed it was their father. He had a mean streak, Leonard Bute, that was for sure. Men like that often do. It's like a part of them knows that they're less than everyone else, and they can't deal with it. Pride, you understand? I always wondered if one of them had bumped him off in the end. Wouldn't have blamed them either."

Was Leonard's death suspicious? Mary made a note to look it up later. Motive and opportunity, according to Ronnie. Mary was feeling more and more like she might be in an episode of Miss Marple. She wondered if Bernie would consider giving Ronnie an honorary WWC membership.

"What about Mrs Bute's death? Did you find that suspicious?"

Ronnie looked surprised by the question. "Not at all. It was funny, I'd wondered if she would come out of her shell once Leonard finally passed on. And she did for a little while. Started wearing make-up and all sorts. Then she got together with that Lynford fellow and that was a total disaster."

"It was?"

"Yes. He ran off and left her, didn't he? And worst of it he left that little mouse of a girl with her. She made the other two kids look like social butterflies, I can tell you that. People used to say she was stupid, or other, worse words. Nowadays they would probably find her a diagnosis. Anxiety, maybe. I've never seen a kid look so scared of her own shadow."

"Were you surprised that they left so soon after their mother died?"

"Not at all, if I was them I would have wanted a fresh start too. You might have guessed, but I didn't think the woman was a very good mother. More interested in the men in her life than the kids. It's no wonder that Michael turned out how he did."

Mary leaned forward. "What do you mean by that?"

For the first time, Ronnie looked uncomfortable.

"Well, I just mean the rumours… They didn't have a chance, did they? Not with a mother like that."

"What rumours?" Mary asked.

"I really couldn't say. It was such a long time ago."

Mary could see the woman wanted her to leave it there, but she knew she had to keep pressing.

"Was there ever a suspicion in the neighbourhood that Mrs Bute's death might not have been natural? Especially given what you said about her children?"

"No."

"You don't think they would have a motive for murder?"

"They would hardly kill their own mother, would they?" Ronnie struggled to her feet to indicate the interview was over.

"They just might," Mary muttered, but the elderly woman pulled her cardigan around her and pretended not to hear.

Mary left Ronnie's house and watched the woman pull the

curtains tightly across the front window. She had a feeling she had disturbed the old lady more than she had meant to. It wasn't nice to think that your neighbours might have been murderers. Or that you might have ignored the warning signs at the time. Mary wondered if it was partly guilt that made Ronnie shiver when she mentioned the Bute family. Perhaps if someone had intervened, if some neighbour had said something then the family could have had a happier outcome.

She got into her car and headed back to pick up her kids. There was nothing Mary could do for the Bute children as they were thirty-odd years ago. But maybe she could solve a crime and put someone to prison that had avoided it for decades. And that would be some measure of comfort, to her at least.

Chapter 12: Walker

Walker walked along the street with his gun out. The sniper rifle was across his back. A sound made him turn and he noticed the group of men approaching him, night-vision goggles adorning their faces. He raised his gun in the exact second that they took aim.

His phone rang.

"Are you playing that shooter game again?" Mary's voice said as he fumbled to turn off the telly.

"No," he lied.

"You were meant to tell me so that we could team up!"

"Yeah, I forgot."

"Liar," Mary laughed. "I wasn't that bad last time, was I?"

"I spent the whole time reviving you. And you refused to shoot the angry wolves."

"Kill the puppies? Are you mad?"

"They were fiery hell-hounds…" Walker paused, then laughed, "I can never win an argument with you, can I?"

"Nope. Listen, I need to talk to you about WWC stuff. I know that you said the only file for Michael Bute was the traffic offence, but I had an idea. Apparently, he was a bit of a nightmare at school, so I was wondering if you could check out if young Michael had any official run-ins with the police. Macleod didn't seem to think so, but judging from what the neighbour told me, there might be something on his record from when he was a kid."

"Those records are expunged when you hit eighteen," Walker reminded her.

"Yeah, but someone must remember what he was up to, or there might be some unofficial paperwork kicking about somewhere."

"I guess I could try," Walker said, not sure how he would go about it, but knowing he would at least look into it. It was getting increasingly hard for him to deny Mary Plunkett anything.

"Did you try what I said about getting to know your new Constable?"

Walker walked over to the fridge and pulled out a beer. "Yes. I've invited him for a drink after work tomorrow. He said he was up for it, so we'll see."

"Is he very handsome?" Mary asked. "I mean, I might be looking to upgrade to someone younger."

"He's definitely younger. He looks like he should still be in High School."

"Jealous?"

"Not a bit," Walker said. "He's definitely not your type. He had never heard of *Supernatural*."

"You're kidding!"

"Nope."

"I suppose I'll keep you then."

At that moment the doorbell went. "Hang on there's someone at the door. Speak later?"

"Sure," Mary said, hanging up the phone.

Walker went to answer the bell and saw that Constable Williamson, who Walker knew a little from the station, was standing at the door.

"Everything okay?" Walker asked. Police officers were just like members of the public in that respect: no good ever came of an unannounced visit.

"Yes." Williamson couldn't have looked more awkward if he had tried. "I live just a couple of streets away and I remembered picking you up from here once. I… um, I was wondering if I could have a word?"

Intrigued, Walker opened the door and showed him inside.

"Everything all right?" Walker wished he could remember the man's first name. Unfortunately he could only remember his office nickname, which was Hand Luggage, due to his tendency to go on holiday multiple times a year. The worry etched into Williamson's face told Walker that it would be inappropriate to call him that right now.

79

"I think I might be in a bit of trouble," Williamson said once they were inside. "I'm sorry to bring this to you, but I was hoping we could have an unofficial chat about it before I go into the office tomorrow morning."

"Of course," Walker said, pleased that the man felt he could come to him. "How can I help you?"

"It's about Lucas Duncan."

Walker couldn't hide his surprise. Mary had told him about Liz's case, but as far as he knew it was an old mis-per that had been closed long ago.

"You've heard of him then," Williamson said, clocking Walker's expression.

"I know that my girlfriend's agency is investigating him. His partner says she hasn't heard from him in eighteen months."

Williamson shuffled his feet. "Yeah, I heard about that. The thing is, I was the one that took the initial missing person's report."

Ah, now it made sense. "And that's why you're here."

"Yeah. I think I screwed up. I never thought for a minute that he was anything other than voluntarily absent. And now there's a chance that he might not be."

"As far as I know, the WWC hasn't found any evidence of foul play."

Williamson's mouth was still turned down at the corners. "I

hope to God they don't. But whether they do or not, someone is going to take a look at the initial investigation and find out that… well, that there wasn't any."

"Why don't you tell me exactly what happened," Walker said.

"It was his partner that came in. The whole thing was a bit off from the start. She wasn't sure if he was missing or not, he had taken his passport but not told her he was leaving… She came across as unreliable and I wasn't sure anything she was telling me was the truth. When I pushed her, she said that he had threatened to leave before, even gone through with it for a few days at a time and then come back."

"So you thought he'd done that again?"

Williamson nodded. "There was precedent for it. I still made a note on the system and listed him as missing. But I never believed it. The thing is, I knew the guy. Not well, but he used to hang out with a group of troublemakers that hung out around the Abbey at the weekend. Nothing too bad, a few cautions for affray and public nuisance. Weeing in the alleys, that sort of thing. I just thought he was a regular loser."

Walker didn't say anything. He wanted to be sympathetic to Williamson, but it was clear that he had gone into this case with more than a little prejudice against Duncan.

"And then the next day we got a call from his mother-in-law. She said that she didn't know why her daughter was reporting him missing, that they had had a row and he had gone off perfectly willingly. It fit with everything we knew about the guy. I put a note on the file and after a couple of weeks when we didn't hear anything we closed the case." Williamson swallowed. "I mean, I closed the case. But now I'm thinking I shouldn't have taken the mother-in-law's word for it, right?"

"Probably not," Walker said, trying not to rub salt in the wound. He could see where Williamson was coming from, but it did seem like he could have done a bit better.

"I hadn't even thought about him since then, but on Friday some of the guys were talking about your girlfriend's private detection agency and how they had been asking about Duncan."

Realisation dawned. "So part of the reason you came here was because I know the people in the WWC?"

Williamson nodded. "Yeah. I've heard that their boss is a bit of a hard case."

"She makes hard cases look... well, soft," Walker said, rather lamely.

"That's what I heard. I'm worried that they're going to make trouble for me over this. I know I should have followed it up, but I don't deserve to get any formal sanction for it, do I?"

Even Walker had no idea about that one. "Just tell the boss everything you told me. First thing Monday morning so that you're pre-empting any inquiry. Honesty still counts for something."

"Right," Williamson said miserably. "And what about the WWC?"

Walker shrugged. "I'll have a word with them. Despite appearances, they can be discreet. You wouldn't believe how many secret affairs they've discovered. If I tell them that you've already fessed up to your mistake, they probably won't try and make things any worse for you."

"Really?"

"No promises, but I would think so."

"Well, that's something," Williamson said. He didn't look much comforted. There was nothing worse than knowing you had screwed up and just having to wait for the inevitable bollocking.

Williamson left soon after that, leaving Walker to ponder his fate. There would definitely be a telling off, but probably nothing formal. After all, missing people were reported every single day and most of them did turn up. Lucas Duncan wasn't a vulnerable person and he was over eighteen so he wouldn't have been a priority case.

If it turned out that a criminal act had been committed, that might change things. And in that case, Williamson would have to face not only his boss but Bernie Paterson as well. Walker wouldn't wish that on anyone.

Chapter 13: Bernie

It was late on Sunday night and Bernie still had to fit in a meeting with the other members of the WWC. This case that Macleod had given them was far too important to coast their way through, so she wanted to check that the others were on the same page.

She dropped off a takeaway with Finn and Ewan – just because she didn't eat it herself, didn't mean that she understood the male need for the occasional kebab, especially when she wasn't around to cook them a nutritionally complete dinner – and got back in the car to head over to Liz's place.

Her phone buzzed just as she was about to start the car.

"Hi, Bernie, it's Walker. I wanted to talk to you about Lucas Duncan."

"Our missing father? That's Liz's case."

"Oh, I'll give her a call then," Walker said. He sounded relieved, but Bernie wasn't about to let him off that easily.

"Why exactly are you calling about him? I didn't realise the police were still investigating."

"They're not. Um. That's sort of the problem." Walker went on to tell her what his constable friend had told him about Mrs Robinson phoning the station and the lack of follow-up on Lucas's disappearance.

"Sounds like a typical police cock-up to me," Bernie said when he had finished speaking.

"Bit harsh," Walker argued. "Look, the lad that took the case probably should have done a bit more, but he only followed procedure."

"You'd be amazed at the amount of work our organisation gets because the police force only followed procedure," Bernie snapped back at him.

"So glad we had this call," Walker said in a snippy tone and Bernie felt it was time to hang up.

Fuelled by indignation, Bernie drove around to Liz's house in record time. When she got there two of Mary's kids had passed out on the sofa.

"I can't stay long," Mary said, covering the kids with one of Liz's cashmere throws. "They're going to be a mess at school tomorrow if I don't get them to bed soon.

Bernie and Liz shared a look. They both had a more relaxed view of bedtime than Mary did, but then they didn't have to wrangle four of the little monsters to bed at the same time.

"All right, let's go through what we've found out."

They went through to the kitchen where Liz prepared some drinks. Bernie stuck to a straight gin with ice as there was a weird carrot smell that was putting her off anything more exotic.

"The more I find out about the Bute family, the more they

seem seriously screwed up," Mary said. She explained what she had found out in the interview with Ronnie, the neighbour.

"That tallies with what the social worker told me. Mrs Cookes was pretty defensive, but it seemed like they could have done more for those kids. Although she did seem to think that Joyce was taking care of Katie at least. Mrs Bute was a waste of space by the sound of things."

"Not really a reason to kill her though, is it?"

Bernie stroked her chin. "I don't know about that. Look how quickly they left to start a new life once she was dead. How are we getting on with finding new addresses for them all?"

"Walker helped me out with that one," Mary said, checking her notes. "There was a record of Michael Bute being pulled over for a traffic offence. Nothing serious, but it did list a current address for him. This was eight years ago, but he was reported as living in a caravan park not too far from here."

"Did you check it out?"

"They're not answering the phone at the moment. I'll try again tomorrow and if I don't get anywhere I'll take a drive out after school."

"Great," Bernie said, pleased that Mary was taking the initiative. "Do you need childcare?"

"No, Matt and Stephanie are coming down for a few days. They've booked an Airbnb so they can have the kids over and do the school run."

"Wow, how did you persuade them to do that?" Liz asked.

"Stephanie offered. She's started sending me all these videos about 'co-parenting' and 'step-mums forever'. It's nice really."

"Is it?"

Mary let out a giggle, covering her mouth as she did so. "Don't get me started, Bernie, I'm determined to see it as a good thing. And the kids are super excited about staying in a fancy cottage. Peter has already planned every takeaway they are going to order over the next three days."

"I thought Stephanie was vegan."

"Flexitarian, at the moment. Pizza is flexitarian though, isn't it?"

"Don't see why not," Bernie said. "Back to the case, I want to find out more about how Mrs Bute died. I've texted Macleod and he says he can get me a meeting with her doctor tomorrow so that might give us some idea whether or not there was anything suspicious about her death."

"I can't believe they didn't do an autopsy."

"It's not like on the telly," Bernie explained. "Most of the time at the care home there isn't any need for a post-mortem. I guess with Mrs Bute having a documented heart condition it was the same thing. But you can bet I'm going to grill the doctor about it. Any news on Lucas Duncan?"

"Not so far," Liz said. "Fiona is turning out to be a total flake. It turns out that Lucas sent her an email just after he disappeared, telling her sorry and that he hoped Marco would be okay."

"Sounds a bit like a suicide note," Mary said.

"Yeah, I wondered about that, but according to Fiona and her parents he sounds a bit too self-obsessed for that. I'm not ruling it out though. I'm definitely going to take a good look at Fiona's parents. Her dad told her off for hiring us."

"Told you she was a drip," Bernie said.

"I know. But she's keeping us on the payroll for the moment, so I'm happy enough to keep looking, at least for the next few days."

Bernie checked the time. It was getting late even without taking the kids into account. "Let's call it a day. Macleod's case is the priority, but I don't mind you spending a bit of time on Lucas Duncan if Fiona is still paying. Let's do this!"

She punched the air. The other two stared at her.

"Sorry, I've been watching American football with Finn. I guess the coaching style doesn't really work in Invergryff."

"Not really," Liz said.

"Sorry. Maybe we could do a cheer or something?"

"Let's just drop it," Bernie said.

She drove home from Liz's and by the time she got out of her car it was so late that Bernie just wanted to fall into bed. But as she was walking up the drive her neighbour, Mr Canning appeared from behind the wheelie bins like a baddie in a videogame.

"You're home late," he said.

"Looks like it," Bernie replied, keeping walking. The man was a terrible bore.

"Still doing that detective thing?"

"Yes," she replied. "I've just come back from a WWC meeting. That alright with you."

"You haven't changed that name yet?"

"What, the Wronged Women's Co-operative? Why should I?"

"Isn't it a bit, you know, sexist."

Bernie gave her a perfect eye-roll. "I'll tell you what, when the majority of our clients are men crying their eyes out that their wives have gone off with their money, or beaten them up, or gone out drunk and never come back, then I'll think about changing it."

"A bit stereotypical."

"Not in my extensive experience," Bernie replied. She was tired of the conversation. There was nothing as dull as people that wouldn't face facts when they were so evidently true.

"Thing is, my mother's cat has gone missing and –"

"Goodnight," she said, walking into her house and shutting the door behind her. Some people just couldn't take a hint.

Chapter 14: Liz Monday

Liz drew in a deep breath and pulled the blazer tight across her boobs. "God damn baby chub," she said as she squeezed the fabric tightly enough to get the button done.

Isioma chewed on her knuckles.

"This is your fault," Liz said to her daughter with a mock-frown.

"Glah?"

"I used to be a size twelve before I had you. Okay, maybe a fourteen but who's counting." Liz checked herself in the mirror. Overall, she was happy with the image. She'd had to iron her old business suit which she hadn't worn since she left her accountancy firm. And she'd put on her most stylish wig. It was the first time in a while that she had worn anything that didn't have baby sick on it, so that was a win in itself.

She checked the time. Just a little after ten. Sean was at school and Dave was downstairs watching the telly. He had dropped his work days so that she would be able to do some part time work for the WWC, and they had managed it without too many arguments. If she wanted to go back full time, however, that would be a different matter. Liz knew that Bernie and Mary considered her rich, but the problem was that with a big salary came a big mortgage. Since she had given up a lucrative career in finance, they had definitely had to tighten their belts, even if it didn't look that way from the outside.

Still, that was a worry for another day. At the moment, she was happy to be a stay-at-home mum, but she still enjoyed the chance to use her brain for the WWC every so often.

Today she was channelling her previous personality: Liz Okoro, corporate accountant. She had arranged a meeting with Mr Robinson, claiming to be from a consultancy business that was interested in working with his firm. This was not entirely a lie. Bernie had told her to make sure her personal website was still up-to-date just in case an occasion like this ever arose. And it was a good opportunity to use a wardrobe full of workwear that was gradually gathering dust.

Mr Robinson's firm had a maintenance unit in the East End of Invergryff as well as two offices, one in Glasgow and one on Invergryff High Street. This seemed to double as an estate agents come letting agency and this was where they had arranged to meet.

Before she went in, Liz took a look at the properties listed in the windows. They were all one and two bedroom flats from the cheaper parts of town. She was surprised at how high the rents were, but then that was the current marketplace. It wasn't hard to see why Mrs Robinson went on so many cruises.

"Can I help you?" A very pretty young woman with huge fake eyelashes was sitting at a desk just inside the front door.

"I've got an appointment with Mr Robinson," Liz explained.

"Oh yes, Mrs Okoro, isn't it?"

"Ms Okoro," Liz corrected. She had never been a fan of 'Mrs', especially when she was working.

"He's running a little late I'm afraid, but I can show you into his office to wait."

"That would be great," Liz said with a smile, letting the woman know there was no offence taken at the 'Mrs'. "Have you worked here for long?"

"Only a couple of weeks, actually," the Receptionist said, showing her into a small room off the main space. It had some horrible corporate artwork on the walls, a desk and four or five office chairs. "I used to work in the Glasgow office."

"A bit quieter here," Liz suggested.

"Yeah, but I've moved to Invergryff now so the commute is much better. Do you want a cup of tea or coffee?"

Liz had already spotted a dirty looking kettle and a tin of instant coffee in the office. "No thank you, I'll be fine."

"All right. Hopefully Mr Robinson won't be too long."

"Good boss is he?"

There was a brief pause. "Of course," the woman said, with a big fake smile. "If you need anything else then let me know."

Not a good boss, then, Liz thought as the woman closed the door. That was interesting. She sat in the silent room for a few moments, before getting up off her chair.

It would be rude, really, as an investigator not to have a quick look around. She nipped over to the other side of the desk and started opening the drawers as quickly and quietly as possible. The top one was locked, and Liz wasn't about to try and break into it.

The next two were unlocked, but didn't have too much inside. Some headed stationery and envelopes, and a few old receipts. Liz was just looking at these when she heard voices from the office. She shoved them into her pocket and nipped back into her seat just before the door opened.

"Mrs Okoro, so sorry I'm late," Mr Robinson said, holding out his hand.

"Ms Okoro," Liz said as she shook it. Robinson was a sprightly-looking older man, probably in his sixties, with the sort of teeth that were a little too white to be real. He had the same cruise ship tan that his wife had been sporting on social media.

"You're here to talk accountancy solutions, is that right?"

Straight away, Liz had decided there was no point in lying. Robinson looked far too canny to be fooled by that sort of thing.

"Actually, I'm here to ask about your son-in-law."

Instantly the fake-charm left the man's face. "What?"

"I'm a private investigator. And an accountant too, by the way. We've been asked by your daughter to see if we can locate Lucas."

"And you thought you would lie your way in here to speak to me," the man said.

"I wanted to hear your side of the story," Liz said quickly. She knew if she didn't persuade him to hear her out she would be kicked out the door in a matter of minutes. "Fiona is convinced that Lucas is in trouble, but I know that you think otherwise."

"Damn right I do," Robinson said, folding his arms across his chest. "Did she tell you just what a stupid sod Lucas is?"

Liz had to hide a smile. She knew that she had him eating out of her hand now.

"Maybe you could tell me why you dislike him?"

"Where do I start? He's been nothing but a leech on my daughter since they got together. Don't get me wrong, she's always been difficult. Always got a cause to fight for and always the opposite of whatever her mother and I believe in. She even protested against fox hunting once. You ever seen a fox hunt in Invergryff? Attention seeking, that's what it is. And that's exactly what she was doing when she got together with Lucas. She picked the biggest waste of space she could find, knowing that we would disapprove of him and she could have her little tantrums."

Liz loved a ranter. They always gave away more than they meant to.

"So you weren't upset when he left?"

"I was bloody well celebrating. I hope he's having the time of his life in Spain, probably knocking up some other poor bastard's daughter."

"Spain? Was there a reason why you were thinking of Spain?"

"He had family over there. A cousin or a half-brother or something. He ran a bar on the Costa del Sol. So we assumed that he had ended up over there. If he was still in Scotland then he would have been mooching around our daughter, looking for money as usual."

"They did have a child together," Liz reminded him. "So it wasn't all about the money."

"You think so, don't you," Mr Robinson said with a sneer. "Believe me, only Fiona wanted that kid. And he's a little monster, you know."

Liz, who had secretly thought the same on her first meeting with Marco was now prepared to defend him to the death.

"He is your grandson."

"One that Fiona has been determined to turn against us. I suppose she told you that we didn't want to see him, is that right?"

Liz's silence was answer enough.

"I don't deny that being kicked on the shins by an out of control toddler is not my idea of fun. But Fiona will only let us meet him on her terms. He must only be served unprocessed food, wear only natural fibres. And then she sits him in front of the telly all day."

Defending Fiona Duncan was becoming more difficult by the minute.

"She is on her own now," Liz said, "I'm sure she would appreciate some more support."

"What, more than paying her rent and bills and everything else she cares to think of?" Mr Robinson's face was turning red. "Look, I know you're trying to help but the best thing that ever happened for my daughter was that Lucas Duncan buggered off out of her life. Fiona might want to find him, but you'd be hard pressed to find any other person who does."

"What if something bad has happened to him?"

Mr Robinson laughed aloud at that. "The worst thing that happened to that boy was that he lost his gravy train. There's no point in you turning this into a circus. He's gone off to Spain or found some other poor lass that doesn't know any better to bankroll his lifestyle. If I ever see him again, then you'll have a murder to worry about."

"I never mentioned the word 'murder' Mr Robinson."

He stood up and opened the door. "That's quite enough now, Ms Okoro. If I find you coming here again under false pretences then you can be sure that I will be notifying the proper authorities."

His raised voice made the young receptionist look up from her phone and hurriedly put it away in her bag. She was looking at Liz with more curiosity now, but Liz just made sure to say a cheerful goodbye on the way out. She had a lot to think about and she knew that despite her frosty interview with Mr Robinson, she would be sure to speak to him again.

Chapter 15: Mary

Scotland didn't have trailer parks. Not like the ones Mary had seen on her favourite American telly shows. There wasn't really the weather for them. But it did have caravan parks and some of them had static 'park homes' that were a similar thing. The more upmarket of these were often retirement communities, and Mary knew there were a couple of them around the river to the west of Invergryff.

This was not one of those communities, which were generally expensive and exclusive. The campsite that had been home to Michael and Joyce Bute was much more at the budget end of the spectrum. As Mary drove through the gates she passed a disused tennis court with nets that sagged to the ground and a duck pond that was fuzzy with green sludge. There were still a few caravans parked up, but the general sense was one of neglect.

The man behind the counter had a thin shirt on that meant Mary could see the hairs on his chest. He had dark hair that was almost certainly dyed: natural hair was never that particular shade of aubergine. He was in his fifties and his grumpy face suggested that customer service was something that happened to other people.

"Hello, I was wondering if I could ask you some questions."

"You don't want to check in?"

"Not today," Mary said, trying for a dazzling smile. "I'm trying to trace some people that used to live here. They were a brother and sister, Michael and Joyce Bute."

The man shook his head. "Sorry, never heard of them."

"According to my sources they stayed here for almost a year. Probably around eight years ago."

"Before my time, I'm afraid," the man said, giving her another joy-less smile. "I only came to work here in 2018."

"Is there anyone here that might remember them?"

"Nah. We don't exactly keep staff for long. I've been here the longest by far and the only other people are the cleaners and they tend to just work a couple of summers and move on. Sorry I can't be more help."

"That's all right," Mary said, although she was disappointed. So many leads in this case had come to nothing.

"Why do you want to speak to them anyway?"

Now, Mary was a generally honest person, but she had learned that the ability to tell a little white lie was sometimes more useful in the pursuit of justice.

"There's a possible inheritance. Some distant cousin or other died and left the family a bit of money. I work for one of those firms that tries to track people down. We take a commission, of course, but there should still be a nice little sum left."

Sometimes the little white lie just happened to be a whopping great fib.

"Is that so?" The man looked a little more animated at this idea. "Pity I can't help you then. Maybe you could leave your details and if I think of anyone then I can pass them on."

Pleased to get at least this minor result, Mary left one of her WWC cards on the counter and headed back to the car. She was glad to exit the building and get out into the fresh air. She checked her watch and saw that she still had some time to kill. A quick glance at her phone told her there was a café just around the corner. Perhaps they might remember the Butes. And there was always a chance of some baked goods to consume.

The village of Macken was just a couple of minutes' drive from the caravan park. By the time she parked the car, Mary had decided that Macken was a bit too posh for her. Most people walking around were retirees and it had a very sleepy feel. The clothing shops she walked past had tweeds in the windows, which was a good clue that everything would be out of her budget.

She ducked into the café that she had spotted from the car. It was quiet, since it was between breakfast and lunch, and she was pleased to see there was a large selection of homemade baking.

A minute later she had found herself a seat in the corner and a lovely apple Danish along with a real tea complete with teapot. Mary had always taken pleasure in the little things and there wasn't much to be said against some sweet pastry and a nice hot cuppa.

When the woman from behind the counter appeared beside her cleaning tables, Mary decided to ask about the campsite.

"I was thinking about staying in one of the caravans," Mary explained.

"Really?" The woman looked surprised, tucking her cloth into her apron. "It's not the nicest place in the world. Bit of a local eyesore. I can recommend lots of nice B&Bs if you're looking for a place to stay."

"It's been there a while, hasn't it?"

"About twenty years. And that's when they last looked after the place, I reckon."

"The guy behind the desk didn't seem very friendly."

"Oh aye, that's Bill Stewart. He's been there a while now. I wouldn't want to get on his bad side, that's for sure."

"Really?"

"Yeah. Bit of a reputation for hitting first, asking questions later. Mind you, as I said it's kind of a tough place so it's not surprising he has to lay down the law sometimes."

"He's been here a while, hasn't he?"

"Longer than me," the woman said. "We only opened up five years ago."

Mary was disappointed. It seemed like no one here had been around at the same time as the Butes. She asked the woman if she knew anyone that had been around longer, but the only ones she mentioned lived in town nowhere near the caravan park.

"You could try Patricia Humphreys I suppose. She's been trying to get that place closed down for years. She might know some of the people that lived there."

"Humphreys?"

"She's a local councillor."

"A paid busybody," Mary said, half to herself but the woman laughed.

"That sounds about right. But she's been here forever so she might have some idea about the people you're looking for."

"Any idea where I can find her?"

"No, but I can give you her number."

Mary wrote the number down. She took a bite of her Danish, happy in the knowledge that she had done enough to justify claiming it on expenses. Another successful day.

Chapter 16: Walker

Walker was treating his new trainee to lunch. He had decided to follow Mary's advice and attempt to befriend the sour-faced Phil Higgins. It was not going all that well.

"Is this place the best Invergryff has to offer?" Phil said, glancing at the menu.

"It's quick and close to the station," Walker said, feeling a defensive pang for his adopted home. Invergryff wasn't a city, but it had all the good points of small town Scotland. All the bad points too, mind you. "The fish and chips isn't bad. Where are you from anyway?" he asked the Constable, trying to make up for his sharp tone.

"Falkirk. I've still got a flat there."

"Are you commuting back and forth?"

"Nah, staying with a girl I know down here."

There was something a little leery about the way he said it, but Walker didn't want to get into the man's private life any more than was polite.

"And what do you think of the station so far?" Walker asked.

"It's fine. Good to be seeing what real policing looks like," Phil said, but his face didn't look quite as enthused as his words.

"I'm happy to take feedback," Walker said. "I mean, we're doing a more individual training than we would normally do, so it might be good to tailor things to what you would like to do."

"I was hoping I might get away from the computer screen at some point," Phil said with a slight edge to his tone.

"But you're so good at the spreadsheets!" Walker laughed. "It takes you two hours to do something that takes me the best part of a week."

"It's been a bit more than two hours already," Phil reminded him.

Walker felt the accusation and couldn't deny it. "All right, we'll see about doing something else this afternoon. How about some on-the-beat policing? Take a wander around the town centre?"

"Okay," Phil said, but again he looked like he would rather be somewhere else. "You want another coke?"

"Sure," Walker said, happy for the excuse to get a break from the man. There was just something about Higgin's sense of injustice and entitlement that rubbed him up the wrong way. Had Walker been like that when he first joined the force? He couldn't really remember, but he sincerely hoped not.

Walker checked his phone. Only three *Doctor Who* memes from Mary. She must be busy working today. There was also an email from Bernie that had been sent to him and Macleod. He decided to read that one later. It always took him a while to build up the courage to read a Bernie Paterson email.

Phil seemed to be taking forever at the bar. Walker noted that he was chatting to a pretty barmaid with a tattoo sleeve and a trendy haircut. He seemed to be doing quite well, judging from the woman's body language. Walker felt a little jealous. He had always been rubbish at flirting. In fact, it was lucky that he had managed to find a woman who considered watching vintage sci-fi together to be top level seduction. Watching Phil smooth back his hair at the bar made Walker more determined than ever not to let Mary Plunkett go.

Eventually, Phil came back from the bar with a couple of soft drinks and a smug expression.

"Get her number?" Walker asked, knowing it was expected of him.

"Yep."

Walker was saved from having to feign interest by his phone ringing. It was Mary.

"Hiya," Walker said. He could have taken the phone outside, but a petty part of him wanted to show Phil that he was capable of nabbing a woman too.

"Hi, I need some help with this case. Did you see Bernie's message to Macleod?"

"Not yet."

"She's stressing because we haven't found any of the Bute family yet. I don't blame her, the caravan park was a bit of a bust. I've got one possible lead, but if it doesn't pan out then I'll still be struggling to find where Michael and Joyce went after they stayed there."

"Have you tried the electoral role?"

"No success so far. Don't think they took an active interest in politics somehow. And I've got absolutely nowhere with Katie Lynford. I was wondering if you could do a search for me. She wasn't at the caravan park with the other two, so she's disappeared between leaving Invergryff and the caravan park a couple of years later. Maybe try the extended Lynford family?"

"I'll need to check with Macleod but as long as he okay's it, I'll take a look for you."

"Thanks. Are you still coming over for dinner?"

"Definitely. I'll bring the wine," he said, mainly for Higgin's benefit.

"Not the fizzy stuff, it makes me bloated," Mary said, a little too loud. "See you later!"

"Were you talking about work stuff to your girlfriend," Higgins asked once Walker had put down the phone. "Isn't that a bit cheeky?"

"There are special circumstances," Walker replied. "She works for a private detective agency and she is working a cold case at the moment."

"Your girlfriend is a private investigator?"

"That's right," Walker said.

"And she's working on an active criminal case?"

It was Walker's turn to feel uncomfortable with the conversation. "It's not quite that simple. As I said, she works for an investigative agency and they are employed to work on this cold case."

"Is that allowed?" the Constable asked.

Walker shifted in his chair. "Macleod has sanctioned it. The WWC are official consultants now so… it's one of those things that seems to work best if you don't question it."

"The WWC? What does that stand for?"

"I forget," Walker lied, and he changed the subject. The thing was, Walker wasn't entirely comfortable with the role of WWC either, but he had learned over the past couple of years that they had a value that the official police force couldn't match. And if it meant that murderers and other criminals were brought to justice, then it had to be worth the odd uncomfortable conversation. Including this one.

"It's funny that they didn't send you out with the next set of recruits," Walker said when there was a pause in the conversation. "I mean, no one has actually told me why you didn't graduate with the rest of your cohort."

"I failed the fitness test," Phil said. His neck was bright red now.

"Ah, plenty of people do that," Walker said. Funnily enough, he'd never had a problem with doing any of the exercises that the police training put him through. The written tests on the other hand were a particular type of torture.

"Yeah," Phil said, tracing his finger in a pattern on the table. Walker waited a minute to see if the man was going to offer any more information but he wasn't opening up any further.

There was still some sort of story there, Walker thought. Failing a fitness test wouldn't normally delay your graduation from the college. There was something Phil Higgins wasn't telling him.

"Hadn't we better get back to work?" Phil asked, already reaching for his coat. Yes, there was a story there and Walker was determined to get to the bottom of it.

As they were going out they saw a woman walking along the street throwing bread to the birds.

"Ah, here's an opportunity to meet one of our local characters," Walker said.

"Are you serious?" Phil looked horrified. "Can't we just leave her be?"

"I'm not going to arrest her. I'm just going to check if she's eaten. Her name is Valda and she's homeless most of the time, unless she's managed to get a few nights in a hostel."

"She's feeding the birds," Phil said.

"Yes?"

"I hate birds."

Resisting the urge to ask the man if there was anything on this earth that he actually liked, Walker made his way over to Valda.

"How are you doing today?"

"Good sir," she said. Walker had told her his name several times, but he wasn't sure if she just forgot it or wasn't interested. He didn't blame her. For people like Valda, a man in a uniform wasn't normally a friend.

"Eaten anything lately?"

"Had some bread," Valda said, gesturing to the meal she was currently providing for the town's flying rats.

"Anything else."

Valda shrugged and threw another handful of crumbs on the ground. Unfortunately these landed right where Phil was standing, causing him to jump backwards with a womanly shriek.

"Really?" Walker laughed.

"I hate birds," Phil said, but for the first time, Walker saw him crack a smile.

"Only idiots hate birds," Valda said, wiping the smile from Phil's face as quickly as it had appeared.

Walker reached into his pockets and hunted around until he found a chocolate bar.

"Here, take this?"

Valda snatched it out of his hand. "Thanks," she said, then shuffled off along the street, following by her hopping band of followers.

"Birds, huh?" Walker said as they headed towards the station.

"Let's not talk about it."

Strangely enough, it made him like the man a little better. At least when he had been running from the pigeon he hadn't been pretending to be cool, or acting like he was better than everyone else. It was nice to see something of the real Phil Higgins.

Chapter 17: Bernie

Bernie was sitting in a doctor's waiting room, thinking about how it was one of her least favourite places to be. She was a healthy person. After she had passed through her big weight loss transformation – which she used to call 'shedding the elephant skin' until Liz told her that it was a) offensive and b) gross – she made the effort to be healthy in every aspect of her life. Part of that commitment was to avoid spending any time at the GPs with its waiting room full of germs and viruses.

Someone coughed behind her and Bernie moved chairs, giving the elderly gentleman a glare as she did so. Some people had no consideration for others. Thankfully it wasn't long before her name was called and she went in to meet Doctor Ian Black, a man about her own age with a stubbly chin and a blue shirt that showed sweat stains at the armpits.

"Sorry to have to get you in like this," he said as she sat down. "I simply don't have any other time in the day. This is technically my lunch-hour."

Bernie would have had more sympathy for him if she hadn't spent her time in the waiting room doing an online search to find out how much GPs got paid.

"You wanted to talk to me about Mrs Bute," Dr Black prompted.

"I do. I have a letter here from Detective Inspector Macleod to say that it is part of a police investigation, so you needn't worry about all that Hippocratic Oath nonsense."

"Nonsense?" The Doctor began, but Bernie didn't want to waste any of her fifteen minutes so she went right on talking.

"You were Mrs Bute's doctor when she passed away, is that correct?"

"I was her GP, yes. I'd been seeing her for around two years. Before that, it was Hettie Smith, but she retired."

"You saw her often?"

"She had a few health conditions that needed regular check-ups."

"Which were?"

The Doctor paused.

"Remember I have a signed document from the police station at Invergryff saying that I'm an official consultant, if you're worried about it," Bernie said quickly.

Dr Black checked his watch and Bernie wondered if his lunch-hour was more important to him than his desire for confidentiality. "She had arthritis, mainly suffering pain in her knees and hips. She would have probably needed a hip replacement at some point and that was something we had discussed." The Doctor typed something into his computer and peered over his glasses to look at it. "She also had some mental health issues, low mood and anxiety reported several times. She was keen to try medication but I had suggested alternative methods for the time being. And then there was the heart complaint."

"That's what was listed as the cause of death, is that right?"

He nodded. "She had an arrhythmia. We were monitoring it, but we didn't believe it was bad enough to require further action such as a pacemaker."

"Must have been a bit of shocker for you when she died," Bernie said.

"I hope that you are not insinuating I was at fault," the Doctor said, pursing his lips. "These sorts of heart conditions can worsen suddenly. It's just one of those things."

"And there was no post mortem. I must admit I find that surprising," Bernie said.

The Doctor shrugged. "There isn't always. Rule of thumb is that if there is an obvious medical reason and she was seen by a doctor within two weeks of her death, a post mortem might not be in everyone's best interests."

"And if it turns out that she was murdered?"

"Then there may well be an inquiry. But we are all only human, Mrs Paterson. We are all fallible."

"Some more so than others, but by the looks of things," Bernie said.

The Doctor checked his watch. "I think that's time up."

Even Bernie could read that sort of signal. She left the GPs with more of a spring in her step than she had gone in with.

There was no concrete evidence, but it seemed possible to Bernie that Mrs Bute could have been killed and no one in authority would have noticed it. Now she just had to prove them wrong.

When she came out of the GP's office she noticed that she had a missed call from DI Macleod. She phoned him back immediately.

"I had a request through from Walker about the Lynford family. He said that you wanted some searches done to see if Katie Lynford had any relatives that we missed."

"That's right," Bernie said, phone pressed to her ear as she climbed into the car. She made sure not to turn the engine on, just in case the copper could sense if she was going to have her phone on while driving. "We've found out one of the places that Joyce and Michael Bute went after their mother died was a caravan park in Macken. They were there for a couple of years, but it doesn't sound like Katie was with them."

"And you've no sign of her since then?"

"No."

"All right, I'll get Walker to look into it. But I can't spare too many man-hours on it. The whole point of having the WWC investigate was so that I wouldn't be pulling resources from active cases."

This felt like a dig, and Bernie was about to say something cutting back when Macleod claimed he had a meeting and hung up the call.

"Rude!" Bernie said aloud. Honestly, the police had the case for a decade and did nothing with it, but just because they hadn't found the answers in five minutes Macleod was giving her flak? She decided she would give the man a piece of her mind the next time she saw him.

But there was no point in worrying about it right now. Hopefully, Walker would dredge up something on Katie Lynford. She knew that Mary at least seemed to be getting somewhere with the Bute siblings. If only Liz's case wasn't such a washout. Bernie hated waste and the Lucas Duncan case had waste-of-time written all over it.

She drove towards the gym in the East End of Invergryff. It had taken her several years but she had finally found a spin bike class that wasn't just for wimps. She still had to shout at the instructor sometimes if they looked like they were flagging, but it was a good use of an hour. And she could work out some of her frustrations about Macleod too. Probably better than doing it to his face.

Chapter 18: Liz

It was Tuesday lunchtime and Liz had arranged to meet Mary to chat about the Lucas Duncan case. Or to moan about it, to be more accurate, as she didn't feel like it was going well. Because it was Mary they had arranged to meet in a café in the centre of Invergryff that did afternoon tea.

"This is not going to help me get back to my pre-baby body," Liz said, loosening a button on her blazer. She wished she had thought to change out of her suit.

"Nonsense, you look amazing," Mary said, carefully putting clotted cream onto her already jam-coated scone. "After I had Lauren I looked like Shrek for the best part of a year."

"Liar," Liz laughed. "I've seen the pics. You look exactly the same as you did before you had four children. I don't know how you do it."

"A healthy diet of chocolate cereal combined with less than four hours of sleep a night and little to no exercise," Mary said with a shrug. "Thing is, we always think we look terrible, but other people think we look fine. It's a weird female thing."

"Maybe," Liz said. "I'd swap looking like Beyoncé for getting somewhere on this Lucas Duncan case at the moment. I feel like Bernie is going to start losing patience with me soon."

"Ah, she did say something about 'Liz and her lost causes' when I spoke to her earlier," Mary said with an apologetic expression.

"See, I knew it. The thing is, she's not wrong. So far I've got no leads on where Lucas might be. I'm also worried about Fiona Duncan. She didn't want to tell me about the email from Lucas, so there's a possibility that he has been in touch and she's just not telling me. Her parents reckon that Lucas was just using her for her money and he wouldn't care one bit if he never saw his son again. Those parents by the way are a piece of work themselves. I wouldn't wish the Robinsons as grandparents on any poor kid."

"What if they bumped him off," Mary said, popping a piece of carrot cake into her mouth. "The grandparents I mean."

"Do you know, I would have said you were crazy even to think so until I started looking into the Robinsons' reputation in Invergryff. They're borderline gangster types. Own half of Invergryff and certainly did not like their potential son-in-law. They don't even visit the grandson."

"That's awful," Mary said. "But not proof of murder."

"Not yet. But there's still no sign of Lucas, despite the supposed emails that he sent saying he was going abroad. No social media anyway, which is odd in itself for a man his age."

"But not unheard-of," Bernie reminded her. "These Robinsons sound like a nightmare, but we still need a more definite lead to follow."

"I know," Liz said, irritated by the reminder, even though she knew her friend was right. "Any suggestions?"

"I'd go back to Fiona Duncan. I'd try and find out if there are any family members that Lucas might have been in touch with. Did you find out anything from his sister?"

Liz shook her head. "You mean Roro Duncan? No. After Sean found her on social media I sent her a message but she didn't reply. I guess I could find out where she works and track her down there."

"Worth a try," Mary said. "What's her social media page again?"

Liz brought it up on her phone and Mary scooted her chair around so they could both take a look.

"Is she wearing a lanyard in this one?" Mary said, pointing at a photo where Roro was showing off 'new hair don't care'.

"Yeah. Let me zoom in." Liz tried to see what was on the badge, but the resolution was too poor. "Damn, I can't read it. Do you think it looks like NHS colours though? It reminds me a bit of the one Bernie had for the care home."

Mary had pulled up Roro's page on her own phone now. "I'm going to check out some of her friends. Look, there's this woman Mona who comments on everything." Some more scrolling followed. "Yeah, on Mona's page there's a photo of them all on a night out and Roro is tagged. This woman Mona lists her workplace as Invergryff Hospital."

"Nurses maybe? The restaurant looks a bit cheap for doctors or consultants."

"Or auxiliary staff? Could be cleaners or cooks?"

"That might be possible," Liz said after another moment of searching. "I think Roro's real name is Roxanne and there's no Roxanne Duncan on the NHS website, which she would be if she was a doctor."

"I reckon this is one to pass along to Bernie," Mary said. "She knows tons of people that work in the hospital. I'm sure she'll be able to track Roro down."

"I'll send her a message. No point in calling, she'll be at a weights class or spin or something."

Liz tapped her nails on the table. It was irritating to have to rely on Bernie to help with this case, but she couldn't see what else she could do herself.

"When do you have to pick Issy up from your mum's?" Mary asked.

"In a couple of hours," Liz said after she had checked the time on her phone. "Mum would take her for longer, but the problem is she never wants to give her back. And he would never say anything, but my dad is one of those guys who doesn't know what to do with babies. Once they're old enough to kick a football about he's okay, but he always looks a bit uncomfortable around the little ones. He basically just wants a quiet life, so a baby kind of ruins that."

Mary laughed. "Yeah, they're not quiet. I remember when Peter was born I wondered if he had permanently damaged my hearing. I don't think he did," she said, suddenly looking a bit concerned.

"Can you hear if they are doing something naughty upstairs when you're sitting in the living room with the door closed?"

"Oh yes."

"Then your mum hearing sounds perfect to me," Liz replied. "Are you going to eat that salmon sandwich?"

"No. I don't like to waste my stomach on the savoury course."

"Give it over here then," Liz said.

While she was munching the sandwich Mary's phone buzzed.

"That's Matt texting. He says that Peter has lost his gym shoes and Vikki has started throwing up after eating three sugar-free banana muffins."

"He's getting the real parenting experience then."

"Yep," Mary said happily. "Honestly, I think this might be one of the best weeks of my life. Poor Stephanie though, she won't know what's hit her."

They shared a smile. It wasn't very nice to enjoy the pain of childless people when they were confronted with the reality of looking after the little monsters. But it was very human. Mary and Liz enjoyed another piece of cake in perfect peace. Bliss.

Chapter 19: Mary

After meeting Liz for some delicious afternoon tea, Mary drove back to the town of Macken to try and track down the local councillor. Luckily, she had spoken to her mum that morning and discovered that Patricia Humphreys' day job when she wasn't being a councillor was running the local garden centre.

As Mary parked the car she turned down her playlist of nineties hip hop and tried to get her mind focussed on the task at hand. She had called Humphreys twice and left two messages, which meant either she had the wrong number or the woman wasn't in any rush to speak to her.

Still undecided on a plan, Mary got out of the car and walked into the garden centre. It was smaller than the chain one that Mary normally visited, but considering she would only go there for the café and not the actual garden supplies, that probably didn't signify much. There was a big covered section where the café and the indoor plants were, then a plastic sheeted area for outdoor items.

It was quiet, with just the odd retired couple pottering about and picking up things in pots. Should she pretend to be looking for some plants? Mary looked around at the variety of green leaves with a slight feeling of panic. She was no gardener. In fact, she was a fabled plant killer, once even killing Johnny's favourite cactus by watering it to death.

Mary picked up something that looked a bit like a rose bush and went over to the checkout area.

"I was looking for Patricia Humphreys, is she working today?"

"Aye," the man behind the till nodded. "She's just sorting through the new delivery at the loading bay. Want me to get her for you?"

"No thanks," Mary said cheerfully. "I'll go and find her." One of Bernie's favourite mantras was to always surprise your enemies. And to Bernie, every single person was a potential enemy. Mary had to admit it was a tactic that often proved useful.

She found Patricia Humphreys checking over an order of tiny green things in cardboard sleeves. Humphreys was tall and rangy, with tanned skin from being outdoors. She didn't look like a typical politician, which probably stood her in good stead with the voters.

As she was waiting to speak to the woman, Mary realised she didn't know what party the councillor stood for. She should probably have checked. Politics weren't really her thing. She hadn't even voted last time, partly because she had only just moved to Invergryff and had no idea who any of the candidates were, but mainly because it had been blowing a hoolie that day and she hadn't wanted her hair to get messed up.

"Mrs Humphreys?" she called, moving over to the woman and putting her best impression of a normal human being on. "I was wondering if I could have a word."

Patricia wiped her hands on her khaki coloured apron. "Is it a constituency matter? You don't look like much of a gardener."

"Really? How can you tell?"

"You've picked up a pot of lilies and you're holding it in front of your white t-shirt."

Too late, Mary looked down and pulled the pot away from her chest. A nice stain of orange pollen had been left behind by the white flowers.

"Damn," she said. "Mind you, should have known better than to wear white."

"Come on, let's go to the back office and we'll see if we can clean it off."

Ten minutes and half a roll of sticky tape later, Mary's top was almost pollen-free.

"Thanks for your help," Mary said as Humphreys handed her a cup of tea.

"No problem," the woman replied. "It's not like we're busy. Too rainy for the gardeners at the moment. What was it you wanted to talk about?"

Mary had decided that she liked the woman, so it didn't feel right to make up a story for her. "I'm a private investigator trying to track down some of your old constituents. They lived at the caravan park a few years ago."

"That caravan park is always contentious," Humphreys said,

perching on a wooden stool. "As far as I'm concerned they've got as much right to be there as anyone else. But some of our more... right-leaning members are dying to get rid of the place."

"It is a little bit run down," Mary remarked.

"True, but it brings in a steady flow of visitors in the summer months. I'm inclined to let it stay."

"It's not the caravan park itself that I'm really interested in," Mary said, steering the conversation back to the matter at hand. "I'm looking for two people that were longer term residents, around eight years ago. Michael and Joyce Bute."

She was pleased to see a flash of recognition cross the woman's face.

"I think I remember the names," Humphreys said. "Though I didn't know them well."

"Anything you could tell me would be useful. I'm trying to track them down for a case we're working on."

"What sort of case?"

This time, Mary did decide to lie. Somehow she didn't think the councillor would be quite as chatty if she mentioned the word 'murder'.

"There's a possibility of an inheritance. I can't give too many details, but what I need is a current address for either of them. They were brother and sister."

"I met Joyce a few times," Humphreys said. "I think she might have volunteered for something. It's hard to recall: I do meet a lot of people in my position."

Mary waited.

"I think… It might have been a mental health charity. Or a woman's health one. One of those charities that provides accommodation for women escaping domestic violence. That sort of thing."

"Do you remember what it was called?"

"No. But I could have a look through my computer at home if it would help?"

"That would be great, thank you. You never met Michael Bute, did you?"

"I don't remember ever meeting the brother. Just Joyce."

Was it just because she was a politician that Mary had a feeling the councillor was lying to her? Maybe it was just natural untrustworthiness. After all, what reason could she possibly have not to tell her the truth?

"Sorry I couldn't be more help," Patricia said, leading Mary out of the office. "Would you like to have a look around the plants? I'm sure I can find you something a little less toxic than those lilies."

"Maybe a garden gnome," Mary suggested. "I can't kill one of them. Probably."

Gnome acquired, Mary headed back to the car. Patricia Humphreys had been perfectly nice and Mary would even consider voting for her, if she ever worked out what party she stood for. But she just couldn't shake the feeling that the woman had been holding something back.

Chapter 20: Walker

Walker was working a night shift on Tuesday, which always left him a bit out of sorts during the day. It wasn't like a week of nights, where you got into the hang of sleeping in the daytime, but just one random night shift. He wanted to show Phil Higgins what it was like to be out on the beat, old fashioned policing style, and that required a walk around the rougher areas of Invergryff in the dark. Hopefully, that would give the young man something to remember, at any rate.

By three o'clock he had cleaned his flat twice and even does his expenses. Bored out of his mind, he called Mary.

"Can I come over?"

"Sure. I'm just installing a gnome on the decking."

As usual, Walker didn't understand anything Mary said, but he was happy to be listening. Fifteen minutes' drive later, he was knocking on her door. Technically he had his own set of keys, but it still felt weird to let himself in. Plus it gave Mary a chance to make sure there was no trouser-less children, which happened more often than you might think.

"Come in," Mary said, as she pulled the door open. "I've got the kettle on. Or are you after a beer?"

"Tea please," Walker said. "I'm on night shift from eight."

Mary put the kettle on. Walker waited until her back was

turned before checking to see if his mug was clean. He had once drank a tea that had been spiked with kinetic sand and he had learned a valuable lesson about children and their ability to get their mess everywhere.

"How's it going with the new recruit?" Mary asked.

"I just don't think we're clicking," Walker said. "I mean, it's not like we have to be best friends or anything, but he seems to resent even having to be around me."

"Maybe he's just a bit embarrassed about the situation," Mary suggested. "I mean, if he thought he was going to graduate with his class and do his training in the usual way, it's a bit of a disappointment for him. Especially if he had himself to blame."

"I still don't get how a fitness test could have messed it all up," Walker said. "Normally you would just pass out with the next class once you caught up. But everyone is keeping shtum about it, so who knows."

"I'm sure he'll come around to your charms eventually," Mary said, kissing him on the cheek.

Walker was less sure, but happy to take the compliment. He was just about to sit down on the sofa when he spied an intruder out of the window.

"What in God's name is that?"

"He's my new gnome," Mary grinned. "Do you like him?"

"He's brandishing a chainsaw," Walker said, horrified. The

little man was far too life-like. It reminded him of something out of *Chucky*.

"They're meant to be sort of cheeky, aren't they? I got him from a garden centre."

"You were in a garden centre? Were the scones nice?"

"Oi, I wasn't there for the baking," Mary said, pinching his arm.

"You weren't there for the plants, were you? I thought we agreed that it was just cruel to keep buying them and watching them die. The kids had a vote, as I recall."

"No, I was there to interview someone. A local councillor who had met one of Mrs Bute's children. I didn't find out much, only that Joyce Bute did some volunteering for a women's charity. Still no idea where either of them ended up after the caravan park. But I did have a bit of luck after that."

"Really?"

"I decided to take a step backwards. The one thing we know for sure is they were in Invergryff when they were kids. So I thought I would try and track down one of their teachers. Someone has to remember them. And because I needed local gossip, I called my mum. She knows a lot of teachers and it didn't take me long to find a few names from when Michael and Joyce were at school."

Not for the first time, Walker was jealous of the WWC's gossip network. He was sure that if the police force had the same resources then their crime statistics would be a hell of a lot better. "And what did you learn from that?"

"Nothing yet. I'm meeting Mr Geffrey this evening for a chat. He was the head of Invergryff High School when Joyce and Michael were there, so I'm hoping to at least get the names of the people they hung around with."

"I'm sorry but I've got nothing for you on Michael Bute's juvenile record," Walker said. "I've asked around and apparently there's a guy in records who might be able to help. I'm waiting for him to phone me back."

"What about the Lynfords? Any leads on them?"

"Not so far. I do have to do my actual police work first, you know."

Mary snuggled up to him on the sofa. "I guess that's true. Pity, really, that's the only reason I hang out with you."

"Is that right?" Walker said, tucking a curl of hair behind her ear. "No other reason at all."

"None," she said, kissing him on the lips.

Of course, at that moment his phone rang.

"Sorry," he said as Mary shuffled along the sofa to give him space. "It's the office."

It was Constable Higgins, to be exact. "Sergeant Mickelson is asking if we could start our shift from four. There's a bout of flu going around and half of the afternoon shift hasn't turned up."

Walker was already shifting his mind into work mode. "Of course. Do you need me to give you a lift to the station?"

"Thanks." Phil hung up.

"You're welcome," Walker grumbled to the 'call ended' screen. "I guess I have to go."

Mary shrugged. "It's no problem. I'm binging *TNG* at the moment. I'm only on the third season so it'll keep me going for a while."

Walker kissed her goodbye. One of his favourite things about Mary was that she didn't complain about his work hours. It didn't take long to drive over to the flat where Phil Higgins was staying. It would have been even quicker if the whole area hadn't been colonised by an astonishing amount of speed bumps.

By the time he got out of the car he felt like he had been in a washing machine. He was doubly glad he hadn't had a beer at Mary's house. Still feeling a little delicate, he rang the buzzer for Higgins.

After a couple of minutes, the constable came down the stairs and they got into the car together.

"Sorry you had to wait," Higgins said as he clipped in his belt. "I wasn't expecting you to be so quick."

"I was just over at Mary's, it's not far from here."

"Oh." There was a definite tone to the other man's reply.

"Something bothering you?"

"No."

The silence irritated Walker.

"Why don't you spit it out," he snapped.

"I took a look at this Wronged Women's Co-operative that she's working for. It seems like they enjoy making the force look stupid. And it didn't take long to find photos of you with them on social media. Doesn't seem like a good idea to me."

"You've been checking up on me?" Walker could feel his temper rising.

"Just wanted to find out what the situation was. I don't want to be involved in anything that could come back to bite me on the ass."

"And you think me dating a private investigator could somehow cause trouble for you?"

"I think it could be considered a conflict of interests."

Walker barked out a laugh. "I'm not a politician, Phil. You know, as a police officer you will work with all sorts of civilians. Forensic experts, tech people, anyone involved in social services or the NHS… the WWC are just another group of them."

"And you are sleeping with one of them."

Walker paused. This conversation was getting out of hand, but he wasn't sure how to bring it back to a safer topic.

"If you're really concerned then you can raise it with DI Macleod," Walker said, hoping that that would be the end of it. For a minute he thought that Higgins was going to say something else, but he just gave a curt nod.

"Let's get back to the job," Walker said. "We've got a long shift tonight and I want to go over some of the requirements with you."

The rest of the journey was spent going over procedure. Higgins managed to answer any question correctly, but Walker could tell that neither of their minds was on the upcoming shift.

If things didn't improve soon, Walker thought, then he was going to see if he could get the lad a transfer. Maybe he would find another mentor a bit more suitable. And it might just stop him from killing the lad.

Chapter 21: Bernie

Normally Bernie walked into any room like she was busting for a fight. It was her standard modus operandi – or whatever that Latin phrase was – to enter a room and start causing trouble. But the place that she was visiting today was an exception to the rule.

The old tenement building didn't have a sign outside so only people who knew what it was would be likely to ring the bell. Bernie hit the buzzer for the first floor.

"Hello?"

"I'm here to see Jasmina," Bernie said, looking up at the camera that was hidden in the corner.

"In you come, then," the voice said and the door latch clicked. She made her way to the first floor where a heavy door greeted her. She rang the bell and this time it was opened by a thin woman with pale blue eyes and grey hair.

"Do you have an appointment?"

"Yes, it's Bernie Paterson. I called earlier."

The woman nodded, then allowed Bernie to follow her in. The door was locked carefully behind them. You couldn't be too careful in a women's refuge and Bernie was glad to see that they were taking their security seriously.

She was shown past the main office space into a little side-room with a desk and a couple of chairs.

"Jas is just checking someone in, then she'll be right with you. Would you like a tea?"

"A black coffee please," Bernie said. While she waited she checked over her emails, but there was nothing exciting. Mary had sent a garbled message about a local councillor and some dodgy plants that Bernie would have to read properly later. Liz hadn't sent anything about the Fiona Duncan case, which was proving to be just as much a waste of time as Bernie had thought it would be.

"Hi Bernie, I picked up your coffee," Jas entered balancing two cups and a plate of biscuits along with her work stuff.

"Thanks, it's good to see you again," Bernie said, taking the cup.

"How's the care home?"

"I'm finished there."

"Oh, I thought you were still doing the odd shift."

"Only if they're really stuck," Bernie said, having a sip of the coffee and then vowing not to have another. She had first met Jas when one of the cleaners at the care home had confessed to a particularly horrible home situation. The girl was from Algeria, with pretty basic English and she had come over with a man that was beating her up any chance he got. Bernie couldn't stand that sort of thing. Normally she would have suggested the girl went to the police, but the immigration status was a bit sketchy and she needed another type of help.

A friend of a friend had put her onto Jasmina and her network and they had managed to get secure accommodation for the girl well away from her abuser. Since then they had kept in touch, generally to share a gin and talk about what was wrong with the system that failed so many women. Bernie considered Jas a fellow soldier in the same miserable war.

"So you're full time with your PI thing."

"Yep. There's three of us now, and we're busier than ever. That's why I wanted to speak to you."

"I figured it must be, otherwise you'd have asked to meet at the pub. But you know I'm not going to tell you anything about our women. I mean, even giving you their names could put them in danger."

"Of course. I wouldn't ask you to do that."

Jas took a chocolate digestive and nibbled the edge of it. For once, Bernie didn't even disapprove of the biscuits. She figured that the clients here probably needed a little comfort food.

"We've been asked to look at a cold case by the police. A woman's death ten years ago which was assumed to be natural causes. I'm trying to track down family members and find out if they know anything."

"So what does that have to do with me?"

"I'm getting to that. The dead woman had two children, Michael and Joyce. We've been trying to track them down for the best part of a week. I'm really scrambling in the dark here," Bernie admitted. "The only thing I've managed to learn about the woman, Joyce Bute, is that she might have helped out with a woman's charity around here."

Bernie handed over the only picture they had, which was Joyce's high school photograph, grainy and out of focus.

"I don't recognise her," Jas said.

"That would have been too much to hope for," Bernie replied. "But I thought you might be able to ask around your friends, your co-workers, see if anyone recognises the name, or the person in the photo."

"Maybe she doesn't want to be found for a good reason," Jas said.

"She was a volunteer, not a service user."

"Some of our volunteers are both," Jas explained. "If they have benefitted from our services then they might well come back as a volunteer. I think the same rules of confidentiality would apply."

Normally at this point Bernie would be going off on one, but she was doing her best to be respectful. "I wouldn't ask if it wasn't a serious case. We think someone might have got away with murder."

Jas sighed. "I won't make any promises. But I'll put the feelers out. If anyone knows her, I'll find a way to get her your number. That's as far as I can go."

"Fair enough," Bernie said, even though she was disappointed.

She left Jas to her work and went out of the building, feeling satisfaction as the door locked closed behind her. Some people made fun of the idea of the Wronged Women's Co-operative, thought it was a silly name. But while a lot of their work was men who couldn't keep it in their pants or woman who were obsessed with their co-workers, or any other amount of trivial stuff, this was where the real work was. Violence and danger. Those were just as relevant to the lives of the women who had to come to places like this as they ever were.

And Bernie was determined to dedicate her life to making woman's lives just a little bit better. If that meant she got to kick the arses of a bunch of useless manbabies, then that was just a bonus.

Chapter 22: Liz

The last time Liz had visited Invergryff hospital was when Dave had managed to break his toe playing golf. They had sat in A&E for nearly six hours before being told to go home and let it heal up by itself. Six weeks off the golf course and a lot of male sulking later, Dave was good as new. Liz was glad that this time she would be a little quicker, although she had taken a magazine in her bag, just in case.

According to the message that Bernie had sent her the night before, she was heading to the maternity ward. It took her a little while to get in, especially as she wasn't an official visitor so she had to wait for someone going out for a ciggie break before she could slip in the door. She found her quarry on the third floor where the corridors were dimly lit in the vain hope that the new mums might be able to get some sleep.

Liz was relieved to learn that Roro Duncan went by Roxanne in real life. Roro sounded like something you would name a puppy not a human being. Mind you, Liz thought as she watched the woman clean the corridors of the Invergryff maternity unit, there was something puppy-like about Roxanne Duncan. She wasn't much like her brother. Small and round with blond hair that was growing out of a bob, she was continually moving, making sure the floor sparkled.

"I can't tell you anything about him," Roxanna said straight away. "I don't know why you're here."

It had taken a lot of convincing for the woman to speak to her at all. Bernie had pulled some strings with her network of hospital staff and promised the woman two shifts off if she gave Liz fifteen minutes of her time.

So far it was not proving fruitful. "You're not in touch with him?"

"Not for years. He thought he was too good for the lot of us, especially when he started dating that posh girl."

"Fiona?" Liz definitely hadn't thought of the young woman as posh.

"Aye, her. Sort of a hippy type, you know? When they started going out she would head around to our mam's and tell her off about the recycling and for eating meat and all that crap."

"Your mum doesn't know where Lucas is?"

"Wouldn't have thought so, given she's been dead for two years."

"Sorry, I didn't know."

The mop moved more quickly across the floor. "Didn't even come to the bloody funeral, did he? And that was before he 'disappeared'."

The inverted commas were audible. "You don't think he's really disappeared, then?"

"I think he's gone off somewhere. I don't blame him, that's for sure. Living with Fiona would drive anyone away. But I do feel sorry for the wean."

"Marco?"

"Aye. I've only met him once." The woman's voice wobbled a bit then and Liz couldn't help but feel sorry for her.

"You've not been for a visit since Lucas disappeared?"

"No. Don't think Fiona would want me around, do you? She didn't when Lucas was still around. So better to let it go."

Liz wanted to argue with her, but it wasn't her place. And other people's families were always complicated. Once again she was thankful for Dave and their relatively drama-free life.

"You don't have any idea where he might have gone? Anywhere at all?"

Roxanne kept her head bent down. "No."

"All right, if you think of anything, here's my card."

Roxanne tucked it into her tunic pocket, but still didn't look up. Liz walked back to her car, not feeling too satisfied with her day's work. Roxanne had no idea where her brother was, but she didn't seem to suspect foul play either. If anything, it confirmed that Lucas Duncan was the sort of person who would have no compunction disappearing and leaving behind his family.

On the way home, Liz made a sudden decision to pop by Fiona Duncan's flat. She hadn't updated her client recently, and she wanted to show the woman that she was still active on the case. And a part of her wanted reassurance that she wasn't just wasting everyone's time. After all, if Lucas Duncan was determined not to be found, then there wasn't much she could do about it.

The main door was open, so Liz let herself into the block of flats then made her way up to Fiona's place. Marco's buggy was parked outside, covered in crisp crumbs, so Liz knew they were probably inside.

She rang the bell and after a few minutes Fiona opened the door.

"I didn't know you were coming," she said, glowering at Liz. To be fair, Liz hated unexpected guests as well. They always seemed to turn up when you hadn't done the dishes. When Fiona let her in, it was clear that more than the dishes hadn't been done. There was a pile of clothes on the sofa waiting to be put away and Marco was sat in front of the telly, pulling apart an expensive-looking robotic toy.

"He shouldn't be watching the telly, I know," Fiona said, reaching for the remote. "I don't normally approve of screen time, but –"

"We all do it," Liz said with a reassuring smile. "Even Issy gets half an hour of Cocomelon before bedtime."

"That's the one with the weird dolls and the high-pitched nursery rhymes, right?"

"Yeah, it's the worst."

"Not as bad as some of the stuff on the American channels,"

Fiona said, forgetting to pretend she didn't watch them. "And the ones with talking animals."

Marco was sucking his thumb and Liz was grateful that the screen was saving them from his usual 'boisterous' activity of wrecking the place.

"Maybe we could go into the kitchen while he's busy and have a little chat," she suggested.

With this prompt, Fiona made them both a cup of herbal tea – aniseedy and unpleasant – and they perched on the stools next to the window. A pigeon on the street outside was pecking at the remains of a discarded burger.

"I spoke to your dad," Liz said.

Fiona's mouth turned down at the corners. "Aye, he phoned me."

"What did he say?"

"That some nosy parker had been to his office. You shouldn't have done that," Fiona sniffed.

"It's important that I speak to everyone involved," Liz said sternly. She wasn't about to let the woman tell her how to do her job.

"Dad's not involved."

"He didn't like Lucas much though, did he?"

"No," Fiona narrowed her eyes. "What are you getting at?"

"Well, it pays to consider if anyone might have had a motive to do your husband harm."

"Do him harm? Jesus, you don't think Dad would have hurt him do you?"

"From what I've heard about your dad, he's kind of a tough guy."

"Yeah, he's the worst kind of capitalist scumbag. He thinks nothing of having tenants evicted at a moment's notice. And he's never paid a penny of tax in his life. But he would never actually hurt someone himself."

"What if he got someone else to do it?" Liz pressed. "He must know the sort of people that might be happy to use their fists."

"I see what you're saying, but I don't believe it. The whole reason they didn't like Lucas was that he dragged their perfect little social media image down into the dirt. Mum is all about appearances. She wouldn't let Dad go all gangster on him."

"All right, I'll take that on board," Liz said, without exactly conceding the argument. "I'm going to keep trying to track him down, but I'm finding it tricky. Could you work on a list of friends and family for me? I've already talked to his sister, but she didn't seem to know anything."

"That's Roxanne, right? She always thought she was better than us."

"Funny," Liz said. "That's what she said about you."

"She did?"

Aware that she had probably gone too far, Liz said she needed to go. As Fiona walked her to the door she noticed a pile of unopened letters.

"Is this post for Lucas?" she asked.

"Yeah. I don't know what to do with it. I normally just bin it."

"Mind if I take it?" Liz asked, already putting the letters and flyers into her handbag. "You never know, it might be useful."

Fiona bit her lip, but managed to mutter a quiet 'sure'.

Her stolen treasure in her bag, Liz headed back home. When she was back in her kitchen she quickly opened all the letters. There wasn't anything too unusual, mostly scammy letters fishing for money or begging for charity donations. There was one with a bank account mentioned, so Liz filed that one away for later. By the time Dave got home with the kids Liz was feeling much happier. There was nothing like snooping through someone's private correspondence to brighten up your day.

Chapter 23: Mary

Mr Geffrey, the retired Head Teacher of Invergryff High, had the tidiest house that Mary had ever seen. It was actually starting to make her feel nervous. Not a single item was out of place. In the living room, where she had been shown when she arrived, the remote control was perpendicular to the TV guide on the table and there was a perfectly placed coaster in each of the four corners. It was unsettling, not only because Mary hadn't realised that paper TV guides still existed.

The other thing that was making her nervous was that the man was a former teacher. Mary had always been bright, so school should have been a breeze, but she was a terrible daydreamer. This meant that she was continually getting told off for not paying attention, even though her actual school work had always been good. In fact –

"Are you all right, Mrs Plunkett? Only you haven't said anything for several minutes."

Mary blushed. "Yes, sorry. Just gathering my thoughts."

"Would you like a biscuit?"

Normally Mary was the biscuit queen, but she politely declined. The idea of leaving crumbs behind on the cream leather sofa was giving her hives.

"Thank you for agreeing to speak to me," she said once she had taken a very careful sip of tea. "It's been very tricky trying to track someone down that knew Michael and Joyce Bute."

"I'm not surprised." Mr Geffrey said. He had elected for a black coffee that he was using to warm his thin hands. He was probably heading for eighty, but had the straight back and sharp eyes of someone younger. "They always kept to themselves, even as children. Quiet, withdrawn even. You know that there was some social work involvement."

Mary nodded. "My colleague spoke to their social worker, Mrs Cookes."

"Ah, yes, Emily Cookes. We did a lot of work together back in the nineties. You know, Invergryff was a lot more deprived back then. The eighties were a tough time with the shipyards closing and a lot of people left unemployed. In the nineties, the town was only just starting to recover. Yes, we had a lot of contact with the social work department.'

"And Michael and Joyce Bute were two of those cases."

Mr Geffrey nodded. "It was Emily that first brought them to my attention. As I said, no one had taken much notice of them in school at first. I know that sounds bad, but they weren't the sort of kids that got noticed. They were bright enough not to be really struggling with the work, and not badly behaved enough to get in major trouble."

"So why did social work get involved?"

"Because of the mother," Mr Geffrey explained. He paused for a moment and all that Mary could hear was the tick of the clock in hallway. "Emily was worried that she might be neglecting the children. And although they always attended school on time and were clean and tidy, there were some signs that that might have been the case. They were very timid, didn't talk at all about their home life and didn't have any friends."

"But no one thought to take them away from the mother? Or intervene at all?"

"Do you know how bad it has to get for someone to be removed from a parent? No, there simply wasn't the evidence for that. But Emily was still worried and she made a note on their file so that we took a closer interest in them at school. We made sure they each had access to the school councillor, although I don't think they ever went. Joyce might have done once or twice, but Michael never did. I know it doesn't sound like much, but we did what we could."

Mary wasn't too sure about that, but she wasn't going to antagonise the man. Not when he was so happy to dish the dirt about his former students.

"We might have even thought we had dealt with it all quite well, until the change that came over Michael when he hit fifteen."

"A change?"

"It seemed to come about when they acquired the new stepsister. I can't remember her name, I had left the High School by the time she was old enough to attend."

"It was Katie Lynford."

"Katie, that's it. Well, you don't have to be an educational psychologist to understand why someone acts up when a new kid comes into the family. He was jealous of the attention, I suppose, and that's when he started to become more difficult to manage."

"In what way?"

Mr Geffrey straightened a cushion that had somehow become slightly crooked. "It's a difficult age for boys. Some of them get acne, some turn shy, some turn into little tearaways. And some become very big and very strong too quickly and all of a sudden they learn they can use that strength against others. That was Michael."

"He was a bully?"

"I'm not sure that's the right word. Bullies are quite simple creatures really. They pick on the weak and do it over and over because it's easy. Michael was a lot more subtle than that. If what Emily Cookes said about the mother was true, he was simply implementing what he learned at home. Not that that's any excuse for what he got up to."

"Which was what, exactly?" Mary prompted.

"He took a bit too much interest in some of the girls. There were a few issues in class, inappropriate remarks and some physical encounters. Unwanted encounters."

Mary was sitting up straight at this point, staring at the man. "What exactly are we talking about here? Sexual assault? I would rather you didn't sugar-coat things, Mr Geffrey."

"I think we would call it inappropriate touching. Groping, probably. Nothing worse than that, although I realise that is not nothing. But it was more how he was around the girls. Sadly, it wasn't uncommon for the boys to tease the girls and take it too far. But Michael would get almost obsessed with one girl or another. He would follow her around, even follow her home, and then the parents would complain. The girls never wanted to make a fuss, but still, we were concerned."

"Sounds like you were right to be," Mary said.

"Yes. We had a meeting with the boy and his mother. That was a disaster, as you might imagine. Like many parents who neglect their children, Mrs Bute refused to believe there was anything wrong. Still, I think I might have got through to Michael. His behaviour improved after that. Or at least I didn't catch him doing anything, which is not the same thing, of course."

Mary wasn't too impressed. "Shouldn't more have been done? To support the girls involved at least?"

"I like to think it might be now. But this was in the nineties and often these sorts of things were swept under the carpet. Less hassle for everyone if it just went away."

"Less hassle for the school, certainly?"

"You think you would have done better?" Mr Geffrey said, his tone sharp. "Fourteen hundred pupils we had then, from some of the most deprived streets in the whole of Scotland. We did what we could and certainly a hell of a lot more than most of the parents ever even tried."

"I don't doubt that you did your best," Mary said, trying to placate him. "I'm just trying to understand what life was like in the Bute household."

"Pretty god damn miserable, I would have thought. There was something difficult to like about Michael Bute. I can say it now that I'm long out of teaching and no one cares about my opinions anymore, but some kids are just little arseholes, you know? No matter how many interventions you do or extra support or whatever, they just seem to be born with an attitude that means they don't care what they do, and how many people it hurts."

There was something about Mr Geffrey's words that made Mary shiver.

The teacher put down his mug. "You didn't tell me why you were investigating the Butes?"

Mary figured she had nothing to lose with the truth. "We were asked to look into the death of their mother by the police. There is some concern that her death might not have been natural."

Mr Geffrey gave her a smile that made her feel like she had put her hand up and answered a question correctly.

"That makes sense. If you're asking if Michael Bute could have killed his mother, then there is only one answer. A boy like that likes to get his own way. If there was something stopping that, he wouldn't hesitate to eliminate it."

"I don't suppose you would have anything concrete that might help us," Mary asked. "Like copies of the social work reports?"

"From that long ago? Sorry, not a chance. Any information I've got is all up here." He tapped his forehead.

Mary bit back a sigh. She was pretty sure that Detective Inspector Macleod wouldn't be too impressed if her best evidence for a murder were the opinions of a retired teacher. She thanked the man for his time and promised to update him if they managed to find the Butes.

She drove back home, just beating the rush hour traffic and pulled into the drive. She was humming some Tina Turner as she walked up to the front door. With the kids away, she was looking forward to a lovely long bath with candles and a good book.

Just as she put the key in the lock, her front door opened to reveal Bernie standing in her hallway.

"Surprise!"

"Bloody hell Bernie, you nearly made me pee myself."

"You deserve it. The girlfriend of a copper should know better than to leave her spare key under a plant pot."

Mary's shoulders drooped as she followed the woman into the kitchen.

"Did you clean up in here?" Mary asked.

"Just the surfaces."

"Bernie, you are a real piece of –" The doorbell rang, saving

Mary from saying something that she probably wouldn't regret, but wouldn't do her relationship with her boss much good.

"That'll be Liz. I invited her over for a quick WWC meeting. Hope you don't mind."

"Of course not," Mary said, making an obscene gesture behind Bernie's back as she went to let their friend into the house.

Liz soon redeemed the situation by handing over a pack of donuts which Mary started happily tucking into while the others chatted about their respective cases.

"How did it go with the teacher?" Bernie asked.

"Michael Bute sounds like an absolute horror," Mary said. "Everything I hear about him shows that he could quite easily have committed murder."

"We just have to prove it somehow," Bernie said. At that moment her phone buzzed.

"Hang on, let me get this." She took it into the hallway where she chatted for a few minutes, then came back into the kitchen.

"You're never going to believe who that was," Bernie said as she clicked off the call.

"A new client?" Mary asked. "Or, maybe someone from the school asking about sports day."

For a moment, Bernie seemed off balance. "Why would they be calling about sports day? It's only February."

"Ah, I might have suggested that you could do some lessons

for them. They were asking for parents to help out with some upcoming events, and I might have volunteered you."

"Is it volunteering when you ask someone else to do it?" Bernie said, her tone icy.

"Oh come on, it's not like I can pull off a leotard. In fact, it's pulling it on that's the problem."

"Who the hell was it, Berns," Liz interrupted, stopping Mary just as she was miming trying to climb out of a leotard.

"It was Joyce Bute," Bernie replied. "She wants to meet me."

Chapter 24: Walker

Walker had spent four hours babysitting Phil Higgins, so he figured he could afford to spend a little time on the Bute case. Mary had asked him to look into Mrs Bute's partner, Joe Lynford, the father of Katie. Unlike the other people involved in the Bute case, there was a police file on the man.

He had been born in 1968 and started getting into trouble in his early twenties, by the looks of his record. A couple of cautions of assault and breach of the peace, with alcohol noted as an aggravating factor.

"Neil, can you take a look at this file? Any idea if any of these arresting officers are still around."

"From the nineties? You'd be lucky," Neil Michelson said, but he took a look at the names just in case "Actually, here's someone that you might be able to get hold of. Sergeant Sutton, he was a lifer, retired maybe five years ago. Invergryff born and bred so I don't think he'll have gone far. I can probably get a number for him if you want?"

"Yes please."

Five minutes later, Walker was on the phone to retired sergeant Jimmy Sutton.

"Thanks for taking my call," Walker said, once he had explained who he was. "It's about an old case. Have you got a minute to chat?"

"Sure, just got home from the bowling club," ex-sergeant Sutton said and Walker could hear the kettle boiling in the background.

"Sorry to disturb you. I wanted to ask you about a person of interest. The name is Joe Lynford."

"Doesn't ring any bells."

"Petty criminal, nothing major, but you were the arresting officer."

"Can you send me a picture of him? I'm better with faces than names these days."

"All right," Walker said. He had managed to find an arrest photo from one of Joe's affray charges, so he went into the files to grab it. It took a further ten minutes while Walker worked out how to send the picture and Sutton worked out how to open it.

"Oh yeah, I remember him now," Sutton said, much to Walker's relief. "Joey, they used to call him, I think. He was just one of your Friday night drunks, you know? Nothing particularly special about him. Not the brightest guy in the world. The sort that is the one holding the brick when all his pals have already legged it."

"You didn't hear about him much after his last arrest in the early 2000s?"

"Not if there's nothing on the files. Sorry I can't be more help. Why are you looking at him anyway?"

"His girlfriend passed away in 2012. There's a suggestion that her death might be suspicious and we're taking another look at the case."

"I'd be surprised if Joey was involved," Sutton said. "He didn't seem the type to go around killing people."

"He had a caution for assault."

"Aye, a fight after the football where a group of lads were knocking lumps out of each other. Joey was just going along with the rest of them. Never had the brains to think for himself. How did the woman die?"

"We don't know, but they made it look like a heart attack."

"Definitely not our Joey. I could see if he lost his temper and thumped her, but nothing calculated like that. I don't think he's your man."

"Thanks, it was a long shot. If you think of anything else, let me know."

Walker ended the call. He sent a message to Mary with the information – or lack of – on the case. As he did so he tried to pretend that he couldn't see the judgemental eyes of Constable Higgins watching him from the next desk.

At that moment, DI Macleod came in.

"Any news from your friends about the Bute case?" he asked.

"I was just following up a lead for them," Walker explained. "I talked to the arresting officer who had charged Mrs Bute's partner, Joe Lynford with assault a couple of times. But the sergeant didn't think that he would be likely to kill her."

Macleod nodded. "As far as I remember, he'd been out of the picture for a few years before she died. Still, worth following up. Do we have a current address for him?"

"Nothing since he left the Bute house, but he was a bit of a drifter so that's not too surprising."

"It's funny," Macleod said, a frown creasing his forehead, "how many people involved with this case have vanished off the face of the earth. I'm starting to wonder if there's something more going on here."

"You think there might be more deaths?"

"I'm not going to rule anything out. Let's give the WWC a few more days and see what they come up with."

"All right," Walker said.

"Got any chocolate bars on you?" Macleod asked, poking around Walker's desk.

"Aren't you meant to be doing keto?" Walker reminded him.

Macleod pursed his lips. "I wish I never told you that. A bacon roll's keto isn't it?"

"Without the roll."

"Damn." The DI wandered off in the direction of the vending machines.

Walker noticed Phil's eyes on Macleod as he left.

"He gets grumpy when his blood sugar drops," Walker explained. "If he's ever getting on your case, chuck him a chocolate bar and he'll be right as rain."

Higgins nodded. Then he cleared his throat. "I thought you were making it up when you said that Macleod had sanctioned using the private investigators. I guess I owe you an apology."

Walker's eyebrows shot up his forehead. "Oh."

"So I'm sorry," Higgins said, bowing his head over his computer and returning to his work.

A pig flew past the window. Not really, but that's what Walker imagined must be happening for Phil to admit he was wrong. Time to buy a lottery ticket, he thought.

Chapter 25: Bernie

After so long hunting around on social media, it was hard to believe that she was going to meet Joyce Bute face to face. It was, however, a little galling to discover that Joyce was right here in Invergryff.

The reason they hadn't found her was partly because she had changed her name.

"It's Joyce Mackenzie now. I got married. He didn't stick around, but the name did."

The first thing that struck Bernie about Joyce Bute was how much she looked like the picture of her late mother. Even though Joyce was barely fifty, she looked two decades older. Her hair had been dyed brown but had been let go long enough that the silver roots were half-way down her head. She had the sort of pallid skin colour that made Bernie itch to give her a vitamin regime. And a bit of exercise wouldn't have gone amiss either.

When Bernie arrived at the flat she was invited to sit down on a cracked leather sofa but there was no offer of a cup of tea. Bernie wouldn't have drunk one anyway having seen the state of the kitchen, but it would have been nice to be offered.

"What is it you want?" Joyce said as soon as they sat down. "I got a call from some woman I hadn't seen in a decade. I didn't even know she still had my number. She said there was an investigator looking for me and that the woman had a reputation of being a pain in the arse, so I better meet up with her.

Bernie was pleased to see her reputation was enduring. "We've been looking for you. For you and your brother?"

At the mention of her brother's name, Joyce's hands started to shake. "Haven't seen him."

"Since when?"

"I don't know, eight years maybe? I cut him out."

For once, Bernie wished that Mary was there. Mary was the sort of person that people would pour out their feelings to, even memories of the most traumatic events. Bernie knew that she was a bludgeon rather than a scalpel, and it was making the situation tricky.

She settled for: "You didn't have a very happy childhood, did you?"

For a second she thought Joyce might throw her out of the flat. But to her relief, the woman barked out a laugh.

"That's the understatement of the year." Joyce reached for a threadbare cushion and hugged it on her lap. "Yeah, it was a pretty crappy childhood. Jeremy Kyle crappy, you know?"

That was crappy.

"It would be really helpful if you could tell me about it."

"Why? What does it matter?"

Bernie couldn't think of a way of avoiding the truth. "Did you ever wonder if your mother's death might not have been an accident?"

Joyce would have been a terrible poker player. Her eyes immediately dropped to the floor.

"What do you mean?"

"We've been asked by the police to look into your mother's death."

"The police didn't give a crap at the time."

Bernie nodded. "That's true. But one of the officers investigating the case has asked me to look into it. He says he always wondered if your mother might have been murdered."

Now Joyce managed to raise her head to meet Bernie's gaze. "He's not the only one. I've never thought that she just dropped dead. There was too much meanness in her for that. She wanted to live as long as possible and have us care for her in her old age. She would have wanted to live just to spite us."

"You really didn't like your mother."

"She wasn't worth the hatred," Joyce said, the bitterness clear in her voice. "But I didn't hate her as much as he did."

"You're talking about Michael."

"Yes. I've always thought... I always worried that he might have... well, helped her on her way. We both knew where she kept her heart meds, it would have been so easy for him to give her a little extra one night."

"But you never said anything to the police?"

"God no. I was terrified of him. And there was the kid to think about."

"Katie?"

Joyce nodded. "Poor thing. She didn't deserve to be dumped into our crap-show of a family."

"Where is Katie now?"

"I have no idea. After we left Invergryff I gave her all the money I had – not that it was much, Michael always made sure he 'looked after' the finances – and told her to get on the next train south. To change her name and move on with her life. And she did."

"And you don't know where Michael is?"

"You already asked that," Joyce said stubbornly.

Bernie decided to change tactics. "Do you have any pictures of your brother? Or your mum? We've only got the one from her obituary and your school photos."

Again, Joyce shook her head. "I got rid of everything from the past. No photos, nothing. It's better that way. I don't like to hold onto stuff."

"Not even of Katie?"

Again the eyes flicked to the floor. "No. It was for her own good if I forgot all about her. I liked Katie. I tried to look after her. I was like her big sister back then. And even when Mum was getting worse and worse, we were managing okay. There was only one problem."

"Let me guess: the problem was Michael?"

"Yes." She hugged the cushion tighter to her chest. "It was funny, before our dad died we were like a team, you know? Mum never really bothered with us so we just sort of hung out together. And then when mum first got together with Mr Lynford, Michael started to change."

"In what way?"

"He loved him," Joyce said, in a tender way that was completely unexpected. "He loved that man. He was like everything we had wanted dad to be, you know? He actually paid attention to us. Well, mainly to Michael. Started calling him son, that sort of thing. And Michael just lapped it all up. And Katie was little more than a baby. She was like my little doll. It was... a happy time."

"And then Mr Lynford left."

"Yep. Just showed what happens when you rely on someone. All of a sudden he was gone, leaving us with mum just like it was before. Only this time it was a million times worse because we had been lumped with Katie who needed fed and clothed and all the rest of it, and mum was just getting more and more angry about it all. It got to Michael and he changed."

"You need to tell me what he was like," Bernie said. "No sugar-coating, okay?"

"He had always had a temper. When we were kids, Mum always wanted us to be quiet. Not like normal quiet. We had to be silent so that we didn't disturb dad. It was like she wanted us to pretend we didn't exist. So we learned how to do that. Every time we felt like crying or laughing, we learned not to make a sound. I was pretty good at it actually, but Michael had a tougher time. He was a boy, you see, and they're just louder, need more exercise, all that stuff. So when he couldn't make a noise or anything, it all built up inside him."

"He took it out on you?"

"Who else? He could hardly hit mum or dad. I kind of got used to it, I guess. But then when Katie came along…"

"Did he hit Katie too?"

"I protected her," Joyce said, which Bernie knew wasn't really an answer.

Joyce checked her phone. "I need you to go soon. I'm working in an hour, over at the shop across the road. The pay is crap but it's handy and I don't drive. And I pay my bills myself."

Bernie was starting to appreciate the tiny flat with its fusty atmosphere. For Joyce Bute it must have been paradise. Mind you, she could have still run a duster around the place every so often.

"So you're sure you have no idea where Michael might be

now?" Bernie asked.

"I was hoping he might be dead," Joyce said. "That sounds bad, doesn't it? But I haven't heard from him for all these years, so there's a good chance isn't there?"

"I don't know," Bernie said. "People like that… in my experience the meanness in them, that's what keeps them alive. Used to see it in the care home all the time. The lovely old gents, they would pass away quickly, but the mean ones, they would cling on right to the end. Doing it out of spite."

Bernie's brain caught up to what her mouth was saying and she stopped, surprised. She wasn't normally prone to that sort of thinking. It must have been something about Joyce Bute and the dingy flat that was bringing it out in her.

But Joyce was already nodding in agreement. "Yeah, you're probably right. Too bloody minded just to go off and die and make everyone else's life easier."

"Like Katie's," Bernie prompted.

"I told you already, Katie's done fine. I got her out of there before anything bad could happen. The kid is fine."

Whatever you tell yourself to get by, Bernie thought. But something about Joyce's narrative stayed with her, making her shudder in the car on the way home. What a dreadful home for those kids to grow up in. It took twenty minutes of body pump and two protein shakes before Bernie managed to shake the creepy feeling off.

Chapter 26: Liz

Liz was sitting in Glasgow's poshest bar. She wasn't a big drinker herself, so she didn't recognise half the bottles on the shelves, but she knew that the bill was going to be hefty.

Amy White used to work at Liz's company, before they both left. Liz left to join the WWC, but Amy had taken a job at the premier banking oversight firm in Glasgow, Mitchison and Forthwright. Since then she had already been made partner, the youngest in the firm's history. A very useful contact to have, even if she did look like she'd rather have been somewhere else.

"I don't know why I'm doing this," Amy grumbled as she sat down and pulled off her raincoat.

"Because I'm buying the drinks," Liz said. "And I've ordered us a plate of nibbles as well."

The plate of nuts and olives arrived and Amy popped a salted almond into her mouth. "What are you drinking," she asked.

"I'm getting the train home, so I suppose I can have one glass." Liz happened to glance at the prices on the menu. "One small glass, that is."

"I'm going to order a bottle," Amy said firmly. "You better be paying for this on expenses."

"Of course," Liz said, already cringing at future Bernie's face when she handed over the receipt.

Amy took a piece of paper out of her bag and put it on the table. "I really don't think I should be giving you these."

"I wouldn't ask if it wasn't important," Liz said.

"You know I could get into a hell of a lot of trouble for this."

"Lucas Duncan is missing and we need to find him. The only way to do that is to find out where he's been spending his money."

"Without anything as official as a warrant, right?"

It was turning out to be an awkward conversation. Amy was trained to follow the rules, just like Liz had been once. And she genuinely didn't want to get her friend into any trouble.

"If it helps, his wife is concerned about him," Liz explained. "He's been reported as a missing person."

"Well, that might help me not get fired, I guess. Let's just hope it never comes out."

"You can trust me."

"I guess you never told the boss that time I left my work laptop in that Glasgow Wetherspoons."

"Remember when we went back to get it and some huge drunk guy was sitting on it?" Liz giggled.

"How can I forget? I told IT I had dropped it in the office and they gave me a new one, thank god. I don't think I could have used it again, even if it hadn't been bent like a banana."

"You see, you can definitely trust me," Liz grinned. "Although maybe not to stop you drinking pink tequila."

"Ah, it was pink tequila that night?" Amy snorted a laugh. "That explains why I can't remember anything about it."

A waiter came over with the very expensive bottle and there were a few minutes of small chat while they arranged drinks and waited for him to be out of earshot.

"Do you not find it a bit, weird, I guess, doing this job? I mean, it's not like a real career or anything, is it?"

Liz felt a bit offended. "It is a real job. Just because it pays less than being an accountant, doesn't make it any less valid."

"Sorry, I just meant that… well, it's not the sort of thing you go to uni for, is it?"

"That's why I like it," Liz said. "It's not doing the same thing every day. And it's fun. And none of my co-workers are sexist creeps."

"That must be nice," Amy said, the smile returning to her face.

"I know it seems weird, but being a Private Investigator is a proper job. And we know how to handle any information we receive under the strictest confidence."

Amy blew out a sigh. "Okay. I didn't find out much, but I did get a bank account for your missing guy."

She handed over a piece of paper with Lucas Duncan's name

and some bank account details.

"Other than that, that's all I can say."

"I need more than this," Liz prompted. "Please, I know you wouldn't be giving it to me if you didn't have something."

"All I can say is, the bank account is active," she said finally. "All right, I can tell you that. The guy's not dead, judging from the foreign transactions on his account. There was one just yesterday."

"Foreign transactions? From Spain maybe?"

Amy gave her the tiniest of nods. Then she reached for her bag. "That's me done. I take it you will handle the bill."

"OF course," Liz said. It was worth the money. Definitive proof that Lucas Duncan was alive, and most likely in Spain. That was worth the cost of a few cocktails.

Chapter 27: Mary

Mary and Bernie were hiding in Mary's shed. It was not the ideal place for a meeting, as Bernie had pointed out several times. It was, however, much better than trying to have a conversation inside the house as the children had decided to play their favourite game: 90's rave.

"Where did they learn about raves anyway?" Bernie asked as the sounds of Fatboy Slim rang out across the garden.

"No idea," Mary said sweetly. "Anyway, I can't believe you met Joyce Bute! After all this time searching for her, she came to you."

"It was all a bit strange," Bernie said. "She said she wanted to speak to me, then she clammed up when I suggested that her mother's death might not have been accidental."

"Do you think she's a suspect?"

"Nah, too downtrodden to kill anyone I reckon. Terrified of that brother of hers. If there was any doubt, he's now my number one suspect."

Mary nodded. "His head teacher thought he was a nasty piece of work. It sounded like he was harassing girls at the school and they basically did nothing about it other than tell his mother. The school were more worried about their reputation than protecting the girls by the sound of it."

"Nothing changes there then," Bernie said grimly. "If I was in charge I'd have the whole lot sorted out straight away."

"I'm sure you would," Mary said, shuddering at the idea of Bernie being allowed anywhere near a teaching position. The kids would need so much therapy it would bankrupt the council.

"I just wish Joyce would have told me where Michael is."

"You think she knows?"

"She claims not to. Said she hoped he was dead all these years, but I'm not so sure. When you're that scared of someone you make sure you know where they are at times."

Mary bit her lip. "She sounds traumatised. I don't like the idea of pushing her, but if Michael Bute is as dreadful as we think he is, it would be nice to see him behind bars."

"Don't forget we've still got no actual evidence for the murder," Bernie reminded her. "Even if we do track him down, linking him to his mother's death might be another story."

"Maybe Katie Lynford will be able to help with that," Mary suggested. "I wonder if Joyce knows where she is."

"I should say it was fairly likely, given how close they were. She probably reckons she's protecting the woman by not giving me her details. I'm thinking we might have to send in the baby giraffe with the big cute eyes to win her over."

"The what?"

"I'm talking about you. You go in there with your non-threatening fandom-related outfits and your gentle face and the woman will be putty in your hands."

Mary grimaced. "I don't know how you manage to make compliments sound offensive, Bernie, but it's one of your unique skills."

"You're welcome. Are you up for it?"

"I guess so," Mary said, although she wasn't sure if she would have much luck. If Bernie couldn't bully the answers out of Joyce Bute then the lady must be tougher than she seemed.

The song in the house changed to something by The Prodigy and Mary had to pretend she couldn't see her topless son jumping about the kitchen like a crazed baboon.

"I take it the neighbours are out," Bernie said.

"Yes, I checked. I also give them a very nice bottle of wine every Christmas."

Peter came up to the kitchen window and did a Keith Flint devil face.

"Is he all right?" Bernie asked.

"Yeah. I should probably get back in there before they start smashing things."

Bernie followed her out of the shed. "I thought the kids were still with Matt and Stephanie?"

"They needed to pick up some more supplies. Honestly, I

think Stephanie needed a couple of hours of peace."

"Can't think why," Bernie said, raising her voice so that it carried over the top of the dance hits.

"I would invite you in for a cuppa," Mary said as she opened the kitchen door, "but I'm guessing you would rather not."

"You guessed right," Bernie replied. "See you tomorrow."

Chapter 28: Walker

Walker had just got on shift when they got a call through to do a welfare check. He brought Phil Higgins along so that the man wasn't sulking about spending another day fixing spreadsheets. The check was to be made on a woman who lived on the South side of town. A neighbour had reported raised voices in the night and hadn't been able to get her to answer the door that morning.

The block of flats that they arrived at was a traditional tenement building in one of the more run-down parts of Invergryff. The wheelie bins out front were overflowing, and there was the traditional abandoned supermarket trolley parked up on the pavement.

"How often do these welfare checks flag something up," the Constable asked. If anything, despite Walker's efforts at getting along, the lad was becoming less friendly.

"More often than you might think," Walker replied. "Although this one might well turn out to be nothing. It's the elderly people with a week's worth of milk on the step that you have to worry about."

Phil didn't say anything, but Walker could tell he wasn't impressed. Well, if he was expecting all frontline policing to be endless excitement then the sooner he learned the truth, the better.

There was something a little grimy about the block of flats

even before they went in. The main door to the close was propped open, which made his security-conscious heart wince. The woman's flat was on the first floor so at least they didn't have to go up many steps.

Flat three was facing them as they reached the top of the stairs.

"Look at that," Walker said pointing to the flyers still sticking out of the letterbox. He knocked on the door, but there was no answer.

"They could have just been delivered."

"But none of the other flats have still got them," Walker said.

Phil was looking a bit more animated now. "Should I see if the neighbours have seen her?"

"Good idea."

While the other man went to knock on doors, Walker pushed the flyers through the slot and bent down to take a look through. He couldn't see anything other than a dim hallway.

"Mrs Mackenzie? Are you in there?" There was no sign of life. Of course, she could just be out, but Walker had been a police officer for a while now and sometimes you got a sense of what was going on before the evidence of your own eyes.

"The neighbour on the left hasn't seen her since yesterday morning," Phil said. "He didn't hear anything in the night, and the one who called us in the first place is out. Do you think I should call for backup?"

"Yes," Walker said. While the other officer got on the radio, he examined the door. There was just a simple Yale lock. He brought out his wallet and selected his least-used credit card.

"Tell the office that I'm forcing entry in case of threat to life," he said as calmly as he could manage. Then he wiggled the card in the door until the lock gave way.

"Coming?" He asked the Constable whose eyebrows had risen up his forehead at the sight of Walker's little breaking and entering routine. "Don't worry, I'll make sure we don't get in any trouble. Just try not to touch anything as you go in. Walk in my footsteps."

"It's not a crime scene, is it?"

Walker didn't answer this one. It was funny how you could always sense when something was wrong. There wasn't a smell or anything that told him there was a dead body, but he knew it was there nevertheless. Some sort of animal sense that recognised danger.

It didn't take long to find her. She was sprawled on the living room floor, face down in a position that was incompatible with life. He checked her pulse nevertheless, then called out to Higgins to radio it in.

There was no answer from the man at the door. Walker looked up to see Higgins with a sheen of sweat on his face.

"Constable, please step outside and call it in."

With one last wild look at the body, Higgins put his hand to his mouth and ran out of the flat. Satisfied that if he was going to puke he would at least do it outside of the crime scene, Walker bent down towards the body once more.

There were definite signs of a struggle. The back of her hair was dark and sticky, suggesting that someone had hit her there hard enough to kill her. Of course, it was all just guesses before the men in white coats got to her, but she hadn't died a peaceful death, that was for sure.

He straightened up and took a closer look around the room. It was messy, with unopened letters piled on the table and dirty dishes on the mantelpiece. In a room like this it was hard to tell what was the result of a struggle and what had just been lying around before. A job for forensics, Walker thought and didn't envy them.

A piece of white card was sitting on the coffee table, next to an unwashed mug. Walker recognised the logo before he read the name.

Contact Bernie Paterson, it read, then listed a mobile number, an email address and for some absurd reason, a fax machine.

"Crap," Walker said, just as Higgins walked back into the room.

"What is it?" The Constable asked, and Walker was pleased to see that he looked a bit more composed.

"A business card from the WWC. Bernie Paterson was here."

Walker stood up and walked over to the hallway, where there were some unpaid bills sitting on a shelf. "The woman's name was Joyce Mackenzie. What's the bet that's the same person as this Joyce Bute that Mary and the others have been looking for?"

"Sounds likely to me."

A groan left his lips.

"Everything all right?" Phil asked.

"No. I've just realised I'm going to have to interview Bernie Paterson."

At that moment they heard the sirens and they left the room for the forensic experts to do their business.

They opted to wait in the car until Macleod showed up.

"Were you sick in the end?" Walker asked Phil.

"No. But I thought I might be. That's my first one of them outside of when we had to watch the autopsies in college. It's a bit more… real when they've not been, well, cleaned up."

"Yeah. I puked my guts out the first time. It doesn't get better, but it does get easier if that makes sense."

Macleod tapped the window and the other two men got out.

"Is it true that Joyce Bute is dead up there?" he asked.

"Yes. She's known as Joyce Mackenzie now."

Macleod whistled. "Then this is a right cock-up," he said and stormed off towards the flat without another word.

"He didn't mean our cock-up, did he?" Higgins asked.

"I hope not. Got any chocolate bars on you?"

"Nope."

"Then we could be in real trouble."

Chapter 29: Bernie

It was Thursday morning and Bernie was feeling frustrated. After her meeting with Joyce the day before, the woman had stopped responding to messages. She had tried phoning too, but there was no answer. Very annoying. One of the traits that Bernie found the most irritating in other human beings was the tendency to avoid the truth. Bernie much preferred to grab the truth by the scruff of the neck and glare at it until it surrendered.

She left Joyce a final terse message and headed off to the gym to get a quick session in while she was plotting her next moves. The cross-trainer was one of Bernie's favourite places to come up with ideas. There was something about using all your limbs at once that allowed you to free your brain up for other things.

By the time she left, Bernie had decided to go back to Macleod and re-interview the Detective himself. She wanted to find out more about Mrs Bute's death, the way the body was found and the circumstances around it. If only the body hadn't been cremated, her job would be a whole lot easier.

As she drove back home from the gym, Bernie called Mary for an update.

"I'm still waiting to hear if Walker has found anything on Katie Lynford or her father. I feel like if she has the same memories of childhood that Joyce had, then we'll have confirmation that Michael Bute is a certified bad guy. So I was wanting to talk to

Walker about it this morning, but he's not answering his phone."

"I'm having the same problem with Joyce Bute. Who said mobile phones made life better?"

"Pretty much no one," Mary grumbled.

"You're just annoyed because your boyfriend is ignoring you. Maybe you should ditch him for someone who isn't part of the machine, working for the man. Find a nice artist, or a singer, or maybe a landscape gardener."

"You're joking, right?"

"If you like."

Mary sighed. "It wouldn't normally bother me, but we were supposed to be going for lunch. It's not like him to ignore my messages."

Bernie pulled into her street. Outside her house there was a police car with a tall man in uniform standing next to it.

"I think I might have just found him," she said. "Talk later."

Before Mary could say anything else, Bernie clicked off the call and turned off her car engine. By the time she had opened the door, Sergeant Walker was already there.

"Sorry to turn up like this, Bernie," he said. "I need you to have a chat with us."

"What's happened?"

"We found Joyce Bute in her flat."

"Dead." His face told her all she needed to know.

"Afraid so. We'll need to take a statement."

Bernie wasn't often shocked, but she couldn't stop the surprise from showing on her face. "Of course. Do you want me to come into the station?"

"We can do it here if you like."

"That suits me," Bernie said, pleased that she wouldn't lose time travelling back and forth to the station. If Joyce really had been killed – and there was no doubt in Bernie's mind that her death had not been a natural one – then the sooner she got back to the investigation, the better.

Bernie didn't think much of Walker's new Constable. The man had a face like a slapped bottom and he flat-out refused to try one of her raw peanut butter protein bites, even though she explained how much they could help with his complexion.

She managed to get them both to take a black coffee while Walker explained that they had found Joyce dead in her flat just a couple of hours ago.

"How did she die?"

"We think that –" the Constable began, but Walker held up his hand.

"We can't give you any of the details yet, Bernie, as you well know."

"Hang on a minute, this is my case."

"Look, you can take it up with Macleod when you see him, but for the moment I just want to take your statement. What time did you arrive at Joyce Mackenzie's flat yesterday?"

Bernie confirmed to the men that she had spent a brief part of the afternoon with Joyce, leaving her very much alive around four. Then Walker asked what Joyce had told her.

"That is confidential."

"Oh come on, Bernie, give us a break."

"Tell me how she died."

Walker huffed like a small child and crossed his arms, but Bernie wasn't moved. The police always wanted everything on their own terms, but she had her business to run. She hadn't built the WWC out of nothing in just a couple of years to start backing down.

"Was there any sign that she was afraid of someone? You can tell me that at least."

"She didn't say. But she was the sort of person who would jump if a black cat ran past. I wouldn't say she had any *immediate* fear, but like I said, I only met her that one time."

"Right. And there was no one around her flat, no one suspicious hanging about?"

"She must have died pretty soon after I left then," Bernie said. "Do you think someone waited for me to leave?"

Walker wasn't falling for that one. He just closed his notepad.

"I hope you're going to be a bit more helpful as this investigation continues," he said sternly. "It is a murder investigation after all."

"Tell Macleod to come and chat to me," Bernie said. "I'd much rather talk to the organ grinder than the monkey."

Funnily enough, the police officers left pretty soon after that.

Chapter 30: Liz

Dave and Ewan were at work and school and Issy was fed and content in her bouncer on Thursday afternoon. Liz was catching up on the business accounts for the WWC. Despite being a trained accountant, Bernie generally preferred to do the files herself. Control freaks looked at Bernadette Paterson and thought she was a wee bit uptight. But Bernie had a habit of glaring at the accounts and bashing the laptop keys until they submitted, which led to some creative accounting that Liz liked to review before they submitted it to the HMRC.

She was just checking out some new baby things in the sales – it was amazing how many clothes one small child could use – when the doorbell rang.

"I want a word with you." A woman who looked vaguely familiar was standing on Liz's doorstep with her hands on her hips.

"Do I know you?"

"Christine Robinson."

Ah. Fiona Duncan's mother. Now her visit made sense.

"I'm afraid I cannot discuss my business with someone who isn't my client," Liz said.

"I didn't come to discuss anything," Mrs Robinson replied. She had clearly come spoiling for a fight. "I came here to tell you to stop taking advantage of my daughter."

"I'm not taking advantage of anyone, Mrs Robinson. Your daughter asked my firm for help and that is what we are doing."

"How dare you stick your nose into our family business. I guess you caught the scent of money, didn't you?"

"You are not my client," Liz said firmly, "so I don't have to explain anything to you. If you would like to employ me directly then you could ask any questions you want. I can quote you our hourly rates if you like."

"You can cut that attitude out with me, young lady," said the woman who was probably only ten years older than Liz.

"I think it would be best if you left," Liz said, crossing her arms.

"Not until you promise to end this investigation."

"That is not going to happen."

Mrs Robinson actually stamped her foot. "You are taking advantage of a vulnerable young woman."

"Vulnerable in what way? Or are you referring to the fact that she's on her own with a kid with no support from her family?"

"No support? We pay her bills!"

Liz was about to counter back that there was more to being a parent than bankrolling your children, but she bit back her words. At the end of the day, it wasn't her job to tell the

Robinsons what terrible grandparents they were. It was her job to find Lucas Duncan.

"Perhaps you could help me with some information on why your son-in-law went missing. I was wondering if you or your husband knew any more than you were saying."

A flash of pure anger crossed Mrs Robinson's face. "Don't be ridiculous."

"Is it true that you got in touch with the police directly to tell them to stop looking for Lucas?"

Now Mrs Robinson took a step backwards. "Well, I didn't have much of a choice. Fiona was making such a fuss about it, it was getting embarrassing. So of course I went to explain the real situation to the police station."

"And what was the real situation?"

"That he ran off. No big story to it, no great mystery. He found someone else and he left."

"And you have proof of that, do you?"

For a moment, Liz thought she was going to tell her something, then the woman shook her head.

"I'll be talking to my lawyer. You are clearly out to get all the money you can. Not surprising really, with someone of your type living in a nice house like this. You must be used to using other people for everything you can get."

"Excuse me?" Liz said, her heart pounding. But whether or

not Mrs Robinson had realised she had gone too far, the woman turned on her heel and stalked back down the path to her car, a stupidly huge SUV with shiny white paintwork.

Liz let out a long slow breath. That woman was category A crazy, she thought. No wonder Fiona had left home and become a hippy. And a nice dollop of racism to boot. Lovely. She slammed the door shut and went to get a drink.

She had just clicked the kettle on when the doorbell rang.

"That's it!" Liz said, grabbing the nearest heavy object to hand before she opened the door. "I told you to stay out of it."

"Are you threatening me with a breast pump?" Mary Plunkett asked, looking rather surprised.

"Oh. I thought you were someone else."

Mary followed her inside and Liz shared the story of her encounter with Mrs Robinson while they each enjoyed a fancy coffee.

"She never said that to you!" Mary's eyes were wide at the story of the encounter with Christine Robinson. "You don't think she meant…" Mary trailed off.

"Oh I think she meant exactly that. Someone of my type, i.e. black could only be a money grabbing ho-bag to live in a place like this."

"I'm so sorry," Mary said.

"What are you apologising for? You didn't say it."

"I guess I'm sorry on behalf of all white people ever," Mary said and gave Liz's hand a squeeze. "And I'm sorry you have to deal with this crap."

Liz just wanted to move on and not think about it. "What are you getting Walker for Valentine's Day?" she asked, in a blatant attempt to lighten the mood.

"Oh, well, I've got this custom print of us as superheroes, but it wasn't quite how I imagined it. It's more Ben Affleck Batman than Michael Keaton Batman, if you get what I mean."

"I really don't," Liz said. "Are you going out for dinner?"

"Probably not. Getting a babysitter on Valentine's Day is a bit of a nightmare."

"I'll do it."

Mary looked surprised. "Don't you and Dave want to do something?"

"Are you kidding? We've got a baby. My plan was take-away and beers on the sofa and maybe if we're lucky the baby will sleep more than four hours."

"But you won't want a bunch more kids to look after, will you?"

"Why not?"

"Won't it cramp your style?"

Liz laughed. "My style is faded breastfeeding bras and stretchy leggings. Honestly, why don't you and Walker treat yourself to a night out? You guys deserve it."

"Thank you," Mary pulled her into a bear hug. There was an awkward moment when Mary's terrible superhero earrings got caught in Liz's braids, but they managed to sort it out with only a few squeaks of pain.

"Right, now that's sorted we better get back to work. Bernie will be spinning in her grave."

"She's not dead."

"I know, but somehow the image just works. I said I'd send her a quick email so I better update her on the totally crazy Mrs Robinson."

Liz pulled open the laptop and brought up her latest notes on the Duncan case. "Do you know, I'm half regretting taking this one," she said to Mary. "Even apart from the nasty woman on the doorstep, I don't seem to be any further forward with the actual disappearance."

"Do you still think the Robinsons might have had something to do with it?"

"Maybe. I mean, I've just seen that the woman has a temper. But I think I might have to rule out the idea of them being thrown in jail for murder. Sadly."

"I had a friend of mine look into Lucas Duncan's finances. He didn't access his usual accounts from the time he left Invergryff. But she managed to find another account registered to someone with the same NI number. And that account is still active."

"So he's alive?"

"Looks like it. But there's a catch. It looks like the transactions on the account are taking place in Spain."

"Ah. That is a bit trickier."

"Yep. So I'm trying to get through to the authorities in Spain only my Spanish is non-existent. How's yours?"

"Dos cervezas, por favour," Mary said in a dreadful Spanish accent.

"Is that the best you've got?"

"Sorry."

"It's okay. Let's have a wee Sangria before you go home. It might help us work this case out."

A couple of hours later, the Sangria had not helped with the case and it had done little more than give them both a headache. Fiona Duncan would have to wait a little longer.

Chapter 31: Mary

Mary had got home late from Liz's house, had climbed into her *Fraggle Rock* pyjamas and had just put out the light when Bernie had called. Joyce Bute was dead, killed just hours after Bernie had spoken to her. It left a sour taste in her stomach which did not combine nicely with the Sangria. The case had gone from being a hunt for some missing people and a possible murder investigation to a very definite murder investigation in the present day. At least it explained why Walker had been avoiding her calls, only sending a quick message to say that he was working overtime and would call her when he got the chance.

Joyce Bute had been murdered, and it had to be connected to the case they were building against Michael. As far as Mary was concerned, he was the only suspect. But if he was going around murdering people right now, it meant they had to speed up their efforts.

Mary made herself a cup of tea and put an extra spoonful of sugar in it for luck. Then she opened up her laptop and got to work. She was still trying to find out where Katie Lynford might be and now that Joyce was dead, that seemed even more important.

So far, she hadn't got too far with Katie's background check. The most frustrating part was that she hadn't been able to track down a single one of her former teachers. Bernie had told her that the family social worker had visited the Bute household when Katie had been missing school, but when Mary tried to chase it up, she got nowhere. The current office staff at the High School seemed to have no idea how to find things out from more than ten years ago and none of the teachers had been there that long.

It wasn't hard to imagine how all sorts of abuse from the past managed to escape detection. In the end, she went for the simplest solution she could think of.

She put up a post in one of her fake names (Tiffany McAllen, twenty-eight, lover of guinea pigs and American football) on the Invergryff Crowd social media page.

Hiya, hope it's ok to post here, I was at school in 2010 and I was wondering if anyone remembered the funny teachers at Invergryff High? Some really amazing teachers and some nightmares lololol

With a post like that it didn't take long before Mary had a nice list of around a dozen teachers who had worked at the High School when Katie was there. She took that list and sent off a quick email to Mr Geffrey who had been so helpful previously.

Five minutes later he had sent back an annotated version of the list, with notes of how long each of these people worked at the school and how likely they were to have known Katie. There were a couple of teachers that Geffrey didn't know because they had started after they left, but apart from that his memory had come up trumps. Mary decided to start with Ms Annabel Thorn who Geffrey had described as 'a bit of a loose cannon' which immediately made Mary like her.

A few phone calls later Mary discovered that Annabel Thorn

was now working at the Catholic high school just a couple of miles away. She managed to get a personal email for her – thank you to her mother, Nel, and the contact list of the local ballroom dancing group – and asked if she would like to meet up. Ms Thorn emailed back straight away – clearly a quiet day at the school – to say that she was too busy, but she could do a video call later on.

Mary was just doing some research for this when the doorbell rang. It was the postman and he handed over a signed for delivery, then legged it down the path. The poor man was a little scarred after an incident where Johnny had been trying out his new water balloons.

She opened a large letter and gave out a whoop of excitement when she saw that Katie Lynford's birth certificate was inside. She pulled it out and checked that Katie's details matched what they had listed.

The father's name they already knew, Joseph Lynford, but now she could see the mother's name, listed as Valerie Wilson. Straight away, Mary pulled her phone out and searched the birth, deaths and marriage directory. Sure enough, there was a death certificate listed for Valerie Wilson in 2001. Katie's mother had passed away, like they'd been told.

Another thing that was interesting to Mary was that her mother's place of birth was listed as Birmingham. When Mary searched for Wilson and Birmingham, she found a few hits on social media. Could they be possible relatives of Katie's? Maybe they would know where she was. Using one of her online aliases, Mary sent out messages to anyone that looked like they could be related to Katie, using the same story about a possible inheritance.

Just as she was finishing up, Walker rang.

"Sorry I haven't been in touch," he said. "This is the first time I've had five minutes to myself all day."

"That's all right. I guess Joyce's murder has been keeping you busy."

"You heard about that?"

"Of course I did."

"Oh. I'd like to talk to you about it, but it's an active case now, so I have to watch what I say."

"That's okay." Mary didn't press him. She knew that he was in a difficult position when the WWC investigation collided with an official police one, so she didn't want to make things worse.

"I just had to interview Bernie."

"Did she give you a hard time?"

"What do you think?"

"I'm sorry. I love you."

"I love you too. I'll come and see you when I get a chance, but I don't know when that will be."

Mary hung up the call. She wondered if she should have said to Walker that she had a lead on Katie Lynford's whereabouts, but part of her was on Bernie's side on this one. Walker was an awesome boyfriend and potential 'lobster', of course, but the WWC was her job. Why shouldn't the police have to work for their leads like she did? And wouldn't it be more than a little satisfying if they could find Michael Bute before the cops did? The answer to those questions could only be a resounding yes.

Chapter 32: Walker

It was getting late, but Walker's shift was showing no signs of ending soon.

"How's it going with the noob," Sergeant Neil Michelson said as Walker went to the bathroom to splash some cold water on his eyes.

"All right," Walker said with a shrug. He wasn't loving spending his day with Phil Higgins, but he wasn't about to slag him off to another officer. "He's just learning the ropes."

"Got a bit of an attitude problem, so I hear," Michelson said. They walked over to the snack area, both in search of caffeine.

"No one will tell me why he passed out late," Walker said, grabbing a cup of vending machine coffee.

"I heard he was sneaky," Michelson said. "The word going around is that he was a bit too quick to report other officers for falling behind. Got the reputation of being a snitch."

"That's still a bit vague, isn't it?" Walker said. "What was he snitching about?"

"No one will say. But it must have been pretty bad because the whole college has closed ranks about it. Don't see why we've been lumbered with him in Invergryff, unless it was because they didn't want him anywhere near the rest of his cohort."

Michelson went back into the office and Walker was left alone with his hot cup of terrible coffee. He added a couple of sachets of sugar to make it palatable. When he got back to his desk, he saw that Higgins was sitting in front of his computer, rubbing his eyes.

"I've just finished my report on when we found Joyce Mackenzie's body," Phil said.

"Fancy getting some fresh air," Walker said, noting the grey under his eyes.

"All right," Phil replied. To Walker's surprise, when they walked out through Reception Phil pulled out a packet of cigarettes.

"I didn't know you smoked."

"Trying to quit," Higgins said, his surly expression back. "Is that an issue?"

Walker had had enough. "I had another officer say to me about your negative attitude today, Phil. I think you're going to have to make a bit of an effort."

Phil's jaw clenched. "Is that so?"

"Look, the way I see it, you can serve out your time here in Invergryff, keep everything to yourself and not make any friends. And maybe that's all you want. But if you want anything more than that, any hope of a career, then you better tell me what the hell's going on."

The Constable still didn't look convinced. Walker was ready to give up. There was only so much time he was willing to put into dealing with the lad. Then Phil started to move.

"Let's get out of here," Phil said. "You reckon the pub over the way is serving food?"

This was practically a hug from the surly young man, so Walker quickly agreed. Ten minutes later they were sat at a corner table sipping from their soft drinks and eating crisps. The chef wasn't in for lunch until twelve, so it was the best they were going to get.

Finally, Phil Higgins started to talk. "All right, let's get it over with. I guess you want to hear about the college. You know that I failed the fitness test, right?"

"You told me that before."

"Yeah, well, that part was true. It was my own fault. Bit too much to drink the day before the test, and I was so rough I ended up puking my guts up halfway through. So I ended up missing the cut-off to pass with all the lads I had been doing the training with for over a year."

"That must have been disappointing."

"I was gutted. But I went back, signed up to do another three months so that I could sit it again. Only this time I didn't know any of the people and they already assumed I was a bit of a loser."

"I'm sure they didn't think that," Walker said.

"Didn't matter if they did or not, that's what I thought. But I made a couple of friends. The guy I shared a room with, Noah, he was all right. And he was pals with a couple of female officers, Sarah and Jess. And we all started hanging out together, so that was good."

Walker waited silently while Phil talked. If there was one thing policing had taught him, it was when someone was in the mood to run their mouth off, you just let them do it.

"I sort of fancied Sarah, to be honest. But she was one of those hyper-focussed types. Only interested in the job. I asked her out a couple of times, but she wasn't interested."

Walker shifted in his seat. He didn't like the direction this story was going.

"So I dropped it," Phil said and Walker breathed a little easier. "Anyway, we all just hung out together and it was fine. A few idiots in the group, but no one too bad."

He ate a few crisps, then returned to the story.

"Later on in the year we all passed some written test and we decided to have a night out. We were in the bar, everyone had had a few drinks, me included," Higgins said. "That's right, I'm not claiming to be some sort of saint in all this. Anyway, I look over and here's that pretty probationer, Sarah, and our instructor from the college has his hand on her knee."

"Really?"

"Yeah. I watched for a bit. I mean… I couldn't really believe what I was seeing. He was sort of leaning over her, and she was pretty drunk."

"Too drunk to fight him off?"

"That was what I was worried about. She was sort of turned away from him, in a way that any guy should realise is a 'back off' gesture. But the tutor, he just kept on leaning over her, stroking her leg. It was majorly creepy. His hand was getting a little too high up, and she kept pushing it down, but like I said, she was pretty wasted."

"Anyway, it got to the point where I knew I had to step in. I got in between them, and I told him, 'that's enough, sir,' or something similar. I helped Sarah up so that she could get away from him and the instructor called me some choice names."

"Once I got Sarah over to the bar, I called the two female probationers that shared a flat with her and they came and took her home. By this time she was sobering up and getting pretty upset about it all. I said to her that if she wanted to I would back her up with a complaint, but she said she didn't want to make a fuss."

Phil was breathing more heavily, like he was trying to control his temper, even at the memory. "But the next morning I woke up and I was mad as hell. I mean, what if he tried the same thing with someone else? What if it was something he did regularly, but no one ever spoke up about it? So I went and made a formal complaint myself."

"That took courage," Walker said.

"Or stupidity. I made sure not to mention Sarah's name. She had already said she didn't want to make a complaint, so I didn't want to make life any harder for her."

"And what happened next?"

"They brushed it under the carpet. My word against his and I was warned not to bring it up again. Nasty rumours that could tarnish a well-respected officer's good name, or some such rubbish. So I had to let it go. They made up some crappy excuse to put me in a different class so that at least I didn't have to look at the guy again, but it screwed up my graduation schedule."

"And now everyone thinks I did something dodgy. Or they just think I was too lazy to pass the fitness test. I've not corrected them when they've said that because at least it stops people from looking into it any further. But somehow it's me that's come out of it all with the crap reputation. I can't see things working out in the force for me, to be honest."

Walker felt the guy's anger. "Give it a chance," he said. "Once people get to know you, it'll work out okay. Maybe if you told them what happened…"

"I promised Sarah I wouldn't. That's not her real name, in case you're wondering. And I'd appreciate it if you kept it to yourself. At the end of the day, if the force is so quick to judge me then I don't want to be here either."

It was a tricky situation and Walker was feeling pretty damn guilty for judging Phil just like everyone else. He should have known better than to make assumptions about the man. But at least he could make up for it now.

"All right, here's what we're going to do," Walker said, making sure that Phil was listening. "It sounds like you have every right to be pissed off at how the college treated you, but you're not there anymore. You're one of us now, and you need to get the chip off your shoulder."

Phil started to object but Walker held up his hand.

"I know, you're going to say I'm out of order. But whatever happened at the college – and I for one hope that Sarah does put in a complaint one day – you can't let it affect your job right now. You've got a fresh chance to fit in here. And yes, there are problems in the police force. Of course there are. But you can only change them from the inside. If you quit right now, then you let the bullies and the creeps win. How about we give each other a second chance?"

Phil still couldn't manage a smile, but he did put out his right hand.

"It's a deal."

They shook on it.

"Great," Walker said, glad that they had cleared the air. "Now let's go and solve a murder."

Chapter 33: Bernie

Bernie got out of the shower and got ready as efficiently as possible. Back in her larger days, she used to wear a lot of make-up. Now with the benefit of hindsight she could see that it was an attempt at armour, a hope that people would look at her face rather than the body she disliked. Now that she had reinvented herself, she barely put anything on her face other than a sun blocking moisturizer. She was still Scottish after all.

Seeing as she was working, she put a bit of styling gel through her hair. All that Bernie asked from a haircut was that it was out of her face and didn't need blow-dried. At the moment it was short and choppy and if she could be bothered gelling it, it looked quite cool. Or so she had thought until Ewan said it was a bit 'manga', which she reckoned was probably an insult. Still, what did a twelve year old know about fashion.

Some smart jeans and a polo neck and Bernie was ready to go. Today she had several interviews to do that were connected to the death of Mrs Bute and the probable murder of Joyce. Now that another murder had been committed things were heating up. Mary had been almost in tears when Bernie had told her that Joyce Bute had been killed not long after they started investigating the case, but Bernie was more philosophical. Justice had to be done, and they needed to focus their efforts on the killer, not worry about his victims. They were already beyond saving.

She was about to leave when the doorbell rang. At first she

thought it might be Ewan. Despite her best efforts, her son was one of those kids that lost his keys on a regular basis. One day Bernie would find out where the bloody things disappeared to.

Instead of Ewan, when Bernie opened the door she was surprised to see Detective Inspector Macleod.

"I wasn't expecting you until tomorrow," Bernie said as she showed him into the living room. "Would you like a drink?"

"No thank you, I'm not staying."

Even Bernie could tell that there was a certain frostiness in his tone.

"Is something wrong?"

"I need to talk about the Bute case."

"I didn't think you were here to ask for the recipe for my raw nut bites. Although you should, they have the perfect macros."

Macleod blinked, then pretended she hadn't spoken. "I'm here to update you on the status of the case. Since the death of Joyce Mackenzie it is now an ongoing investigation into a suspicious death."

"I would expect nothing less," Bernie said, nodding in agreement. "In fact, I have some ideas about where you might want to start looking. That brother of hers, for starters, not to mention some other family relatives who have so far –"

Macleod held up his hand. "I'm sure you have some excellent theories, Mrs Paterson, but I'm afraid it's time to leave it to the professionals."

"The professionals?" Bernie's lips pursed.

"It's now a police matter," Macleod said. "That is, it is exclusively a police matter. Your involvement must come to an end."

"It bloody well must not!" Bernie rose to her feet. "We were here first!"

"That's not how the justice system works, I'm afraid," Macleod said. "You see, now we have an active murder, we can get the Specialist Crime Division to look into it."

"Well you needn't look so bloody happy about it," Bernie said, her hands clenching into fists. "The poor woman is dead."

"And whose fault is that?"

For a moment, she was almost speechless. Almost. "You can't be suggesting it's our fault."

"I did ask you to be discreet. A cold case more than ten years old, you've been investigating for five minutes and someone gets killed."

"Of all the ridiculous –"

Macleod held up his hand. "Please don't say anything you might regret, Mrs Paterson."

"I never regret anything I say," Bernie replied.

The DI let out a long sigh. "I'm sure you don't. Look, can we just back up a little? I can see you've done an excellent job on this case. And I don't really blame you for the death of Joyce Bute."

Bernie narrowed her eyes. "But?"

"But we now have to think about how things are going to look to the procurator fiscal. I cannot let anything go on that might jeopardise the chance of Joyce Bute's killer getting justice."

"We are nothing other than professional," Bernie said.

"The fact remains that you need to take a step back. You will be paid for your contributions to the case, of course, but that is as far as it goes."

Bernie leaned back and crossed her arms. Her new plan was simply to get rid of the man as quickly as possible so that she could get back to the case. Bernie Paterson had never let anyone tell her what to do and she certainly wasn't about to start with this fool of a copper.

"We have an understanding then," Macleod said as he headed for the door.

"Oh, I understand you perfectly," Bernie said, making sure to slam it shut behind him. She pulled out her phone and tapped in a text.

Urgent WWC meeting tonight. Liz's place, 8pm. Bring gin (lots of). B.

Chapter 34: Liz

Liz was watching the front drive to see when Mary was going to turn up.

"Is that nerd here yet?" Bernie shouted from the kitchen.

"Not yet."

"She's nearly ten minutes late."

The atmosphere in the kitchen was decidedly frosty. Bernie was in a horror of a mood and she wouldn't say why. Liz had given her a drink and then left her in the kitchen, making some excuse to get out of there.

A flash of headlights showed that Mary had turned up. Liz rushed out to meet her friend.

"I came out to warn you," Liz said as she met Mary on the path. "Before you go in there Bernie is on the warpath."

"It's not something I've done, is it?" Mary asked as they walked through the door.

"Better hope not. She's absolutely fizzing."

"Oh dear."

"I've never seen Bernie this angry," Liz whispered, worried about Bernie's bat-like hearing. "Even the time that she found out the care home had been giving her full-fat milk instead of skimmed for a month."

"What's happened?"

"I don't know. She said she wanted you to be here before she talked about it. But she's sitting in my kitchen eating a chocolate chip cookie?"

"A what?"

"You heard me."

Mary's jaw dropped, which was something Liz didn't realise happened in real life. It made her look like a basking shark.

"Not some horrible protein biscuit thing?"

"No, a genuine cookie. From a supermarket."

"Davros on a bike!" Mary said, which must have been a curse in her culture.

Liz was pleased that Mary understood the gravity of the situation. If they had to deal with Bernie in a crisis, the more of them the better. The two ladies entered the kitchen and approached Bernie like a zookeeper would approach an escaped tiger that hadn't had its lunch, only with a bit more care.

"Hi Bernie, how are you?" Mary asked, her voice a note higher than usual.

"Oh, bloody brilliant," Bernie snapped. She had cookie crumbs on her upper lip. "You're not going to believe what happened today."

Liz joined Mary at the other end of the dining table: they had both ensured that they were out of striking distance from Bernie. After a moment's thought, Liz moved the vase that her mother had bought her when she got married. She didn't want it in the firing line in case things got violent.

"Maybe you could tell us about it," Liz suggested, now that the vase was in the cupboard.

"All right," Bernie replied and then she launched into the story of Detective Inspector Macleod and him removing them from the Bute case.

Now it was Liz's turn to be outraged. "But they asked us to investigate in the first place!"

"I know. The whole thing is absolutely ridiculous. I'm going to complain to the Superintendent."

"It might be better to hold off on that one," Mary said, wincing when Bernie turned her glare onto her. "I just mean, this is only one case. We want to keep the door open for them to use us again. If we go off on one, we might sour the whole deal."

Bernie gave her the sort of look that could curdle milk, but then she nodded. "All right, I get your point. Maybe I won't make an official complaint. But I'm damn sure going to let Macleod know exactly how I feel about it."

"That's fair enough," Mary said, looking relieved. Liz wondered if she was worried about how Walker would react if Bernie attacked the police force directly.

"So what are we going to do?" Liz asked.

"Well, we're sure as hell not going to quit," Bernie said. "We're going to show those idiots at Invergryff station that they can't just dump us like a girlfriend who asked for a house key. No, they are going to rue the day that they crossed us."

Liz coughed. "Okay, but specifically in terms of actions, what are we actually going to do about it?"

"We're going to work the case. Find out who killed Joyce Bute, and if it was her brother then we are going to find him too. But before all that we're going to find Katie Lynford, because if we don't find her soon she might well end up just like her stepsister. And then that'll be more blood on the hands of the Invergryff constabulary."

"Good," Mary said, nodding in agreement. "There's too many secrets in that family and the sooner we uncover them the better. After all, we might have a serial killer on our hands if the same person killed Mrs Bute and Joyce."

"A little dramatic," Bernie said, "but we can't rule it out. Whoever killed those two women clearly has a taste for it. And I'm not going to let him kill anyone else."

"I might have a lead on Katie," Mary said. "Or half a lead at least. I found out that she was born in Birmingham, and I've got the name of her mother. I'm trawling the Birmingham social media groups in the hopes that I can find a relative."

"Excellent. And you better make sure that your boyfriend gets us back on this case."

"Oh, I'll do my best," Mary said, dropping her eyes to the table.

Liz kept quiet. She knew Bernie would be upset that she hadn't got any further with the Lucas Duncan case and she didn't want to poke the beast.

"Worst case scenario we can go to the press. I'm sure they'd be interested to know what a cock-up the police are making of this investigation."

"But we're not going to go nuclear yet," Mary reminded her.

"Yes, yes, I'll wait. But I reserve the right to go nuclear if I need to."

Liz and Mary exchanged a look that said 'you always do'. They just had to hope that diplomacy would work its magic before they ended up in a full blown war.

Chapter 35: Mary

Mary normally didn't do housework while the kids were away out of principle. She had so little time on her own that she liked to spend it either working for the WWC or binge-watching shows that the kids found either too scary or too 'old'. But with the kids away with Matt for several days, she had taken the opportunity to tackle the eldritch horror that was the washing pile.

Even though she wasn't generally a fan of housework, there was something satisfying about the clean, fresh smelling washing all collected into piles on the sofa and floor ready to go upstairs. While the antics of Dean and Sam played on the telly in the background, Mary got her life in order. If she worked more hours for Bernie, times like these would be less frequent, Mary thought. But then again, there was probably more to life than TV and ironing. Wasn't there?

When she paused to check her phone she realised that the councillor, Patricia Mackillop, had left her a message, asking Mary to phone her back. Mary did so, even though she had to wait a while for Patricia who was 'dealing with some flowering cacti' according to the male voice on the phone. Mary idly wondered if 'flowering cacti' would make a good euphemism for something until the councillor came onto the line.

"I hope I'm not interrupting anything important," Patricia said.

"Not at all," Mary replied, looking at piles of washing. "In fact, it's nice to get a break."

"Well, I just wanted to tell you that I remembered something about those people you were looking for."

"You did?"

"Yes. It was Michael and Joyce, wasn't it?"

Mary wondered if she should tell the woman that Joyce Bute was found dead, but she wasn't sure if the police had released the name to the press yet and she didn't want to annoy Macleod any more than they already had.

"That's right," she said.

"I don't remember anything about the sister, but I've had a think about it and I do remember hearing that the brother had moved down south. London, I think."

"Really?" Mary's heart sunk. London would be a nightmare to trace someone who didn't want to be found. "Who told you that?"

"Oh, I'm not too sure. I think it was just the story doing the rounds."

Mary tried not to let the frustration show in her voice. "If you could try and remember that would be very helpful for us."

"I'll have a think," Patricia said. "I'm sure it'll come back to me sometime."

She ended the call and Mary glared at her phone for a few

seconds. There was nothing worse than witnesses who were so completely vague that they were less help than the people that remembered nothing. But she made a note on the case file anyway that Michael Bute might be in London. She had no idea how she was going to follow it up, but Bernie would kick her arse if she left out anything that might just be relevant.

While she was on the computer she looked to see if anyone from Birmingham had replied to her messages. So far, she was lucking out, but there was still time.

Mary clicked her tongue. She knew that Bernie would say time was what they didn't have. The truth was, there was a murderer about and Katie Lynford could well be a target. Despite Bernie's protestations, Mary wasn't completely convinced that part of the guilt for the death of Joyce Bute might lie at the feet of the WWC. If they hadn't tracked her down she might still be alive. That didn't fill Mary with joy.

She snapped her laptop shut and looked at the piles of washing. Now she just had to motivate herself to put it all away. But perhaps a cup of tea and a ginger nut was needed first. She closed the door on the living room and went to get a snack. Much more satisfying.

Chapter 36: Walker

"Briefing in five minutes," Neil Michelson said as soon as Walker and Higgins walked into the station. It didn't give them much time to decompress from what had been a frantic morning. Murder investigations were always like this, a mad flurry of activity in those crucial first few hours.

The other members of the Specialist Crime Division, which everyone still called CID, had arrived to give support to DI Macleod. This meant that Walker was pushed down the pecking order.

"Just hang out at the back of the briefing room," Walker told Higgins as they walked through the office. "The guys from SCD will want to be front and centre. Only speak if anyone asks you a question about how we discovered the body. Don't try and push yourself forward, because believe me, they don't like that."

"You want to join plain clothes, don't you," Phil asked.

"Yes," Walker asked. There wasn't much point in denying it. "I haven't got very far. I'm... well, I have some reading and writing issues. Dyslexia they call it these days. And they say it won't count against you, but let me put it this way: no one has been rushing to take me on so far."

"That doesn't sound fair."

Walker shrugged. It wasn't, but he tried not to think about it too much. "I've not been here for that long so I'm still hoping for a transfer at some point. Macleod can normally smuggle me into the case if he's the Senior Investigating Officer and hopefully he will be for this one."

They had reached the briefing room which was already filling up with bodies and the smell of people who hadn't had a chance to shower.

Macleod turned up after a few minutes and went to the front of the room. "Thanks everyone. If you haven't already heard, we have a suspicious death on our hands. Joyce Mackenzie was discovered in her flat this morning and there were signs of foul play. We're hoping they can fit the autopsy in this evening, but from the initial report, it's looking like a struggle and multiple blows to the head."

Unbidden, the image of Joyce Mackenzie's body flashed across Walker's mind. It was a useful reminder of just how vicious the killing had been. It made him more determined to catch the person responsible, and to do it quickly.

He tuned back into the briefing as Macleod was going over persons of interest.

"Our first concern was to track down Joyce Mackenzie's ex-husband, but he's a no go. He's in Poland right now so a solid alibi. He's flying out this evening to do formal identification, so that's something. Now some of you might know that this family was already on our radar. I had been working with some civilian partners to look into a possible cold case. In 2012, Joyce Mackenzie's mother, Elizabeth Bute died. At the time, the circumstances didn't seem suspicious, but I had some concerns. The death of Joyce Bute suggests that those concerns were valid. I'm going to send out a summary of the Elizabeth Bute inquiry, but our main suspect there was her son, Michael Bute. I believe that we should consider him to be a suspect in Joyce Mackenzie's murder."

Macleod's eyes rested on Walker for a second, then moved on. Walker wasn't surprised that the DI hadn't mentioned the involvement of the WWC by name, but he couldn't help feeling offended on their behalf. If Bernie had seen the way that Macleod had failed to acknowledge the work they had put in, then she would have been tearing him a new one.

"As of this moment, we do not have a current address for Bute, but we're working hard on that one. He didn't have a criminal record as an adult, but we know he had some juvenile convictions. The official record has been expunged, but we've managed to get some personal files from the cops involved with him at the time."

The records that Walker had been trying to get for days, he thought, his frustration mounting. Still, he knew better than to say anything, even when Phil Higgins raised his eyebrows. Now was not the time to cause a fuss.

"The juvenile records show that Michael had an unhealthy attitude toward women, with some stalking behaviour and harassment. Nothing that ended with a custodial sentence, but enough to suggest that he might have some anger issues. As I've said, he is considered our number one suspect."

Macleod cleared his throat. "But we can't neglect the basics. There's always a chance that someone else was involved.

We're hoping to get the full forensic report on the scene in the next couple of days. Let's hope they found a nice bloody handprint somewhere for us."

There was a wry chuckle at this from the assembled officers.

"Sergeant Michelson is going to collate the files from the Elizabeth Bute case and add them to the current case folder. Detective Sergeant Suzie O'Connor is going to liaise with the Lord Advocate's office and forensics and keep that part up to date. I'm going to be divvying up the standard jobs: background checks, talking to neighbours and Joyce Mackenzie's co-workers, so check your messages to see what you've been assigned. Remember, these first twenty-four hours are key, so let's make them count."

They filed out of the briefing room and went back to their computers to get started. Walker walked over to speak to Neil Michelson and see if he wanted some help with the family background.

"I had already been looking into them," Walker explained, "as part of the investigation into Mrs Elizabeth Bute's death, so I can send you the files."

"Thanks, that would be a good help. Send me everything you've got and I'll make sure it's all uploaded to the right places. I see you haven't been able to shake off Higgins yet," Neil said, gesturing to Phil who was taking off his coat at the other end of the office. "I can have a word with traffic if you like? I'm sure they'll be able to keep him busy."

"You know, he's kind of growing on me," Walker replied. "I

think maybe we judged him a bit too quickly. He managed okay when we found Joyce Mackenzie's body. And he's not as stuck up as we thought either. I think he might fit in okay."

"If he stops walking around with a major attitude problem," Neil replied.

"Yeah. But honestly, he's all right. Maybe he could come along to the next fives match."

"He can't be much worse than you," Neil laughed. "All right, tell him to come along. If he scores a hat trick for us I might even forgive his grumpy face."

"I'll let him know," Walker said.

At that moment, Macleod walked over and Walker wanted to tell him something that was bugging him.

"You know Joyce's step-sister?"

Macleod nodded. "Katie Lynford."

"That's right. I've been wondering about her father, Joe Lynford." Walker asked.

The officers around them turned to look at him.

"What about him?"

"The family story was that he ran off. And he never got back in touch with his daughter. But I've been looking into him and there's no record of him anywhere since he left the Bute household. Maybe we should check him out. Because if something happened to him, then we could be looking at three murders."

Macleod's face was grim, but he nodded. "All right, add him to the list too. Even if he's not a victim, he could know something. I want every single person connected to the Butes and Joyce Mackenzie checked out."

Macleod headed out towards the snack section and Walker joined him to get a terrible coffee out of the machine.

"That was a good catch about Joe Lynford," Macleod said as Walker tried to get the machine to take his coins.

"Thanks."

"We're not going to have a problem, are we?"

"A problem?"

"Because I took the WWC off the case. I don't think Bernadette Paterson was very happy about it."

"That's not a problem for me," Walker said. "But…"

"But what?"

"Well, I suppose I think that they did quite a lot of work on this case. I mean, without them we would be in a much more difficult position looking for the Butes."

"Without them, Joyce Bute wouldn't be dead!"

"That seems a little unfair."

Macleod shrugged. "Tell me I'm wrong."

Walker tried to work out a way of phrasing things that wasn't going to get him into trouble. "I think maybe you're feeling a bit guilty about her death too and you're deflecting that onto the WWC."

"Thank you very much Sigmund Freud, but I think I know my own mind. Now don't you have work to do?"

Glad for the way out, Walker scurried back into the office before he could dig himself any deeper.

Chapter 37: Bernie

Bernie had driven past Joyce Mackenzie's flat, just to glare at the police cars and the bright white forensic tent outside. Sadly, no one had looked over to see her glaring, but she had done it just in case. It was Friday and it should have been the start of a fun weekend with her family, but instead, she had decided to spend it sulking.

A sulk was not something that she usually indulged in, however, and a couple of hours in she was feeling more than a little bored. How did teenagers summon the strength to sulk for days? While she was pondering that, an email arrived from Liz with the latest updates on the Lucas Duncan case, including his financial records.

It lit a spark in Bernie's mind which led to some frantic internet searching. Half an hour later the sulk was gone and she was back to her old self. She sent a message to the other WWC members and told them to meet at headquarters for lunch.

The house that the WWC used as their office/retreat/gin party headquarters had been kindly gifted to Bernie by a friend who had passed away a couple of years ago. Often it was easier to just meet at one of their own houses, but Bernie liked the idea that they had an official address.

She drove over to the house and made sure that there was fresh milk in the fridge. By the time the other two had arrived,

Bernie had ordered a takeaway with a couple of sub-type sandwiches for Liz and Mary and a protein heavy salad for herself.

The other two arrived and set upon the subs happily. Mary added extra mayonnaise even though Bernie reminded her about empty calories. There was no telling some people.

"I wanted to refocus our efforts," Bernie said once they were all well-fed. "I don't care what Macleod says, we know this case better than anyone. But what I want to focus on is the connections between the death of Mrs Bute and the murder of her daughter."

"We're part of that connection, aren't we?" Mary asked.

"Don't be so maudlin," Bernie reminded her. "But yes, the investigation into her mother's death seems most likely to be the catalyst for her murder. But how?"

Mary put down her sub. "I was thinking about it today and we still don't know who wrote that letter to Macleod. The one that suggested that Mrs Bute had not died a natural death."

"Oh, I'd have thought that was fairly obvious," Bernie said. "It was Joyce, of course. Might even have been the thing that got her killed. She couldn't bear the fact that Michael had gotten away with it for so long. And she thought he was dead, so he couldn't hurt her. No such luck there."

Mary looked surprised. "You're sure it was her?"

"She only had three books in that flat, already going mouldy. They were some of those dreary self-help books for people who can't manage their own lives. Falafel for the soul or how to summon your inner bully or something similar. What a waste of time, the woman couldn't find her backbone even if I gave her a scalpel for the purpose. Anyway, the author was Emmeline Volk."

"Volk. The name of the person who wrote the letter."

"That's right. I don't think Joyce Bute was overflowing with imagination. She needed a fake name and there it was, right in front of her. Of course, if she'd never sent the letter she might still be alive, so it was a poor decision on her part."

"Maybe she just couldn't live with the secret any longer," Mary said. "I mean, if she knew who killed her mother and didn't say anything, it must have been eating her up all that time."

"Aye, but what gave her the push to write the letter? I think something must have brought her mother's murder to mind all these years later. And I reckon that if we find out what it was, it might give us a clue as to what happened to Mrs Bute all those years ago."

"Michael Bute. He's the key. Either the killer or the one telling the killer what to do, I'm sure of it. Mary, I want you to focus on that."

Mary looked surprised. "I thought I was to concentrate on Katie Lynford?"

"Her too. I want you to take over the entire case." Bernie enjoyed the look of shock on both Mary and Liz's faces. And she still had one more wee surprise coming up.

"Because Liz and I have something else to do." Bernie turned her laptop around so that the others could see what she had been up to.

"Are those... Bernie, those look like flight tickets."

"Two tickets to Spain, leaving first thing tomorrow morning."

"What?"

"We're off to the Costa del Sol," Bernie grinned. "It's a shame we didn't have longer to get beach body ready, but we'll have to do."

Liz had crossed her arms. "Bernie, I cannot just jet off to Spain with less than twenty-four hours' notice."

"Why not? You want to find Lucas Duncan, don't you? And those pictures you showed me sure as hell looked like him."

"But... but..."

"But she has a baby," Mary said, filling in Liz's words for her.

"Exactly," Liz said, finding her voice. "And what about Sean and Dave and everything else that I have responsibilities for."

"I've booked Isioma on the flight with us. It was lucky you already applied for a passport for her."

"Yeah, bloody lucky, it was for a trip to see family in Nigeria, not a random work trip. Look, Bernie, I am not jetting off to Spain with a baby at a moment's notice."

Bernie sighed. She hated when people disappointed her. "For

the last time: why not? Surely the whole point of a job like ours is that we can do exactly what we want, when we want? Or would you rather go back to working in an office?"

Liz stared at her for several seconds. "I guess I'm going to Spain," she said in a small voice.

Mary started laughing, and then somehow they were all at it, Liz snorting great big laughs as well.

"Honestly Bernie, you're the best boss ever," Mary said as they calmed down a little. "When is my trip abroad?"

"When you can justify it as a work expense," Bernie said, filling up her glass. "Now let's make a plan for how we're going to find Lucas Duncan. I'm definitely not coming back from Spain empty handed."

Chapter 38: Liz

In less time than she would have thought even possible, Liz was packed, baby things stowed in the hold and sitting on a plane with Bernie and Isioma.

"I hate planes," Bernie said. "When do they come round with the gin?"

"I'm not surprised that you don't like flying," Liz said, pulling her hair out of Isioma's fist for the hundredth time.

"No?"

"It's a control thing, isn't it? And people who like to be in control generally hate flying."

"What's your point," Bernie said, giving her a death stare.

"I just think you're a wee bit uptight," said Liz, master of understatement. "When the seatbelt light goes off you can do some lunges in the aisle. That always cheers you up."

"True," Bernie said. "I could do some yoga. A little downward facing dog would fit."

"Maybe save that one for when you get home."

Isioma started to grumble as soon as the plane took off. Thankfully, Liz had rejected Bernie's offer to bring the snacks, so she had an endless supply of salt-free baby crisps to keep her happy.

"These taste like cardboard," Bernie said.

"They're not for you."

Isioma gurgled with laughter when Bernie pulled a silly face for her.

"You know, I just can't get my head around Lucas Duncan," Liz said. "Imagine leaving your kid, not much older than Isioma and then just never getting in touch again."

"Plenty of men do it."

"And women."

"But mainly men."

Liz counted to ten in her head. "He might have a good reason not to have been in touch."

"Like what?"

She wracked her brains, but there was nothing she could come up with that would excuse abandoning your family.

"I guess we'll have to wait until we speak to him and find out."

The seatbelt light went off and Liz took Isioma for a quick nappy change in the plane's toilet. As always on a flight it felt like wrestling a mongoose in a phone booth, but she managed it without completely losing her temper and they headed back to their seats.

When she got there Bernie was chatting to the female flight attendant.

"It sounds like you should get rid of him as soon as you get back," Bernie said.

"Do you know, I think you're right? I deserve better, you know?"

"Of course you do."

The woman gave Bernie a grin, then headed back off down the plane.

"What was that all about?"

"Just saving another woman from a fruitless relationship with a feckless man," Bernie said.

"I was only gone five minutes," Liz said, shaking her head. Bernie was a force of nature.

"Give me over that baby. It's been ages since I had a cuddle." Isioma scooted happily into Bernie's arms.

The flight attendant reappeared with some complimentary fizzy wine, presumably for Bernie's relationship advice and Liz found that she was enjoying herself. Bernie was right: it was much more fun than working in an office.

By the time they were told it was time to land, Bernie and Issy were fast asleep curled up together. Liz took a picture to send to Mary when they were allowed wifi again. From this angle, Bernadette Paterson almost looked harmless.

Then Liz remembered how the woman had forced her to fly out to Spain at a moment's notice to track down a missing person, not to mention dragging a baby along, and she revised that idea. If her son had been around, he would have said that Bernie had 'main character energy'. But on days like today, Liz was quite happy to be a sidekick.

Bernie and Isioma both woke up just as the plane was coming into land. Then they had to endure the usual palaver of passport control, luggage pickup and all the other everyday miseries that come with air travel.

When they got through to the main area of the airport, Liz demanded a coffee. While Bernie played with the baby, Liz went over the plan she had been working on when they were on the flight.

"All right, I think I've decided what to do."

"Great," Bernie said. "Let's get outside and Viva Espana!"

"You realise that it's peeing down out there?"

"What?" Belatedly, Bernie looked out of the window. There was an almost Scottish downpour going on. "God dammit. All right, tell me the plan."

"We're going to start in this place, just outside Marbella." Liz showed Bernie a map on her phone.

"Why here?"

"Because they have a 'Supporters of Glasgow Celtic in Spain' club. And from Roxanne's social media pages, she's a bit of a Celtic fan. I'm hoping that if she is then her brother is too. And the town is just five miles from the last known residence of this cousin, Paul Beattie."

"Great. Let me guess, it's based in an Irish pub."

"How did you know?"

"I'm clairvoyant," Bernie said, taking the pram from Liz and pushing it over towards the taxis. Liz was left to struggle with the luggage which seemed to have increased in weight since they got on the plane.

"I could go for a Guinness," Bernie said while they waited for a cab.

"Really? Isn't that a lot of empty calories?"

"It's full of iron so it's practically a superfood."

Liz shook her head. Just when you think you've got Bernie Paterson worked out, she surprises you. Kind of like one of those cute little turtles that snaps its neck out and bites off three of your fingers.

They reached the front of the line and directed the taxi to take them to the town where Lucas Duncan had been spending his money.

"It's weird that it's hot and rainy at the same time," Bernie said, glaring at the rain hitting the windshield. "Rain should be cold. It's unnatural."

Liz felt her eyes drooping as they drove through the Spanish countryside. Unlike Isioma nestled in her car seat and Bernie typing messages on her phone, she hadn't had a snooze on the plane.

She must have drifted off for a moment because it seemed to be only seconds later that they were pulling up outside a pub called *The Emerald Isle*.

It was not the sort of place she would have usually brought a small child, and the floor felt so sticky that she decided to keep Isioma in the stroller. Bernie went up to the bar to ask about the Celtic supporters club. The woman serving was in her late fifties or early sixties with grey hair and a bosom that seemed to arrive before she did.

"Ah, I'm afraid it's my husband that runs the club and he's driving the buses today," the woman said in a Northern Irish accent. "Were you wanting to join up?"

"Not exactly," Bernie said. She ordered a Guinness for herself and a white wine for Liz who was appalled to learn they were out of Sangria.

"We're looking for someone who might live around here," Bernie said once the barwoman had given them their drinks. "We thought he might be a Celtic supporter. A Scottish guy, lived near us."

"Half of this part of Spain is ex-pats, even after Brexit. Most of them seem to be Scots or Geordies."

"This guy has been living here for around eighteen months," Liz explained. "His name is Lucas Duncan. I've got a photo here if you wouldn't mind taking a look."

"You really want to find this guy, eh?" The woman looked at

them a bit more closely. "Why is that then?"

"He's left behind some problems back home and we've come to find him," Bernie said.

"Like half the people out here then. Give us that photo." She took a good look. "He does seem to be familiar," the woman said, a sly grin spreading across her face. "Was it just the two drinks you wanted on your tab?"

"Yes. And I guess this would do for a tip, would it?" Bernie asked, putting a hundred euro note on the bar.

"That's about right, cheers," the woman said, disappearing the cash into her back pocket. "I've seen that lad around all right. Usually turns up when the football's on. But I thought his name was Luke, not Lucas. And I don't think you've got the right surname. I'm sure it's Luke Smith."

"Smith. Of course." Bernie and Liz shared a look. If you had to change your identity, it was generally better to go with something better than 'Smith'. Apart from anything else, it showed a lack of imagination.

"I don't suppose you have a home address for Luke Smith," Liz asked.

"Sorry, no."

"That's all right, I'm sure we can do some digging –" Liz said, just as the woman piped up.

"I know where he works though. That place down near the water that does 'Spanish pizza', whatever the hell that is.

Pizza-coca I think it's called. You might catch him there now."

They rushed out of the bar and waved down another taxi to take them to Pizza-coca. Isioma was starting to enjoy herself now, clapping every time they got in a new car. Liz was glad one of them was having fun. The wine was making her stomach bubble and Bernie didn't seem to have factored meals into this trip.

When they arrived at Pizza-coca it didn't seem like an appealing place to eat, even with Liz's stomach rumbling. It was the usual sort of tourist restaurant with a dozen tables outside, their umbrellas flapping forlornly in the wind.

Inside, the place was dead, with only two tables occupied and a bored looking waitress standing looking at her phone. And there, tending bar, was Lucas Duncan.

Chapter 39: Mary

Mary was feeling the pressure. Bernie and Liz had jetted off to Spain – Liz had sent a picture of Bernie looking angelic, which was oddly unsettling – and now Mary was left in charge of the WWC. Not to mention a murder case that they had been explicitly banned from investigating by DI Macleod.

She wondered if it was Macleod's fault that she hadn't been able to get hold of Walker all day. He had been avoiding her calls, and that wasn't like him. The memes she'd sent hadn't got a response either, even when she'd used ones from Firefly which was her sixth favourite sci-fi show, but Walker's number one.

The kids were due back later that day, which was another worry. Matt and Stephanie had managed a little too well for her liking. There had only been a couple of panicked phone calls, mainly for lost school items and missing coats. One memorable call had occurred when Peter had convinced Stephanie he was allergic to blueberries right after eating a muffin, but Mary just had to explain her it was her son's peculiar sense of humour and there were smiles all around. Well, she assumed there were as she hadn't actually seen their faces.

Who had killed Joyce Bute? Or Joyce Mackenzie, as she was known at the time she died. That was one question. And the other, more uncomfortable question to ask was: had she been killed because the WWC had been poking around. That seemed to be what Macleod believed, and Mary had to admit it seemed plausible. But the wheels had been set in motion by the letter from 'Mrs Volk'. If Bernie was right and Joyce had sent it, then she had brought about her own death. It didn't make Mary feel much better, but it did sooth her conscience a little.

It wasn't until her phone started buzzing with a video-camera icon that Mary remembered she was meant to be having a video call with Katie Lynford's former teacher, Ms Annabel Thorn.

"Hello?"

At first Mary could only see the top of Annabel Thorn's head, then she managed to tilt the camera so that her entire face appeared. Mrs Thorn was slim with dark brown hair that might have been dyed, but could still be natural. She was a few years older than Mary and looked exhausted.

"Sorry if I'm a bit late. It's prelims at the moment and I've got hundreds of the bloody things to mark. Is that a Winnie the Pooh sweatshirt?"

"Yes it is."

"Awesome. Tigger was always my favourite."

Mary knew then that she and Ms Thorn were going to get on just fine. Mary started off by explaining that she was trying to trace Katie Lynford, a former pupil.

"Can I ask why you're looking for her?"

It didn't seem right to use the 'inheritance' lie now that Joyce was dead. "I'm a private investigator. Katie's name came up in a case we're working on, and we're worried that she might be in danger."

"In danger?"

"Her step-sister has been murdered."

Ms Thorn flinched. "Oh dear, would that be Joyce?"

"That's right."

"I met Joyce a couple of times. She would come and pick Katie up after school in the car if it was raining. I saw her more than I ever saw the stepmother."

Mary could hear the disdain in the woman's voice.

"We've been told that Mrs Bute wasn't a great mother to Katie."

"Or to her biological children, from what I could tell. Her son had a bit of a reputation around the school, I don't know if you'd heard that."

"I talked to Mr Geffrey and he said that Michael had behaved inappropriately with some of the girls."

"That was when he was at the High School. By the time I started at Invergryff, Michael and Joyce had left and it was just Katie that was still in school. But there were stories about Michael Bute even then, and when I saw how Katie acted I was worried about his behaviour."

"What was it about Katie that worried you?"

Ms Thorn sucked in her cheeks. "You must understand that I didn't have any proof. I wouldn't like it to go around that I made false accusations, you understand."

"This conversation is purely for background," Mary said, reassuring the woman. "You don't have to worry about your name being involved in this."

"All right. I taught Katie science, but I was also her guidance teacher. That meant I was meant to provide pastoral care. Of course, the problem with that is that the kids have to tell you if there's something wrong. But I could see the signs. Katie always seemed tired, very withdrawn, didn't make friends easily. And there was the mum who never signed any permission slips, always made some excuse why she couldn't manage to come along to parent's evening, those sorts of things. So I made a little time for Katie at the end of one session and asked her if there was anything wrong at home."

"What did she say?"

"That everything was fine. Well, that's a bit of a red flag in itself. Most kids have something about their parents that they don't like, even if it's just that they won't let them watch telly all night. But according to Katie everything was just perfect."

"So what happened next?"

"I made a social work referral. It was difficult as I didn't have any proof of abuse or neglect, but I asked them to go around and check on her just in case."

"And they did?"

"Yes. But it was the same story. Mrs Bute didn't seem to care much about her kids, but she didn't starve them either. The brother and sister were on their best behaviour and it was all happy families when the social worker went round."

"I guess you had no choice but to drop it," Mary said, thinking it was the same old story with the Butes: no one did anything about it.

"What the hell makes you think that?" Ms Thorn snapped back. "Of course I didn't just let it lie."

"Oh. Well, that's good to hear."

"I couldn't do much about her home life, but I decided that I sure as hell could make her school life better. So I made my class a sanctuary for the girl. I let her eat her lunch in the room when the other kids were being mean to her and I made sure she could stay late and do her homework in the hall if she didn't want to go home. And all the while I fostered a love of science in her."

"Wow." This was a whole new side of Katie Lynford that Mary hadn't been aware existed.

"We did a college application for her. She was bright, you see. She could have considered university as well, but there wasn't the money for that of course. When she finished up in school she had to get a job – the mother wouldn't let her 'waste her time' on more full time education, of course – but she was doing night classes. It was all going well, and then her stepmother died."

"That must have been difficult."

"Yes. Not because she loved the woman. I don't think there was any affection there by the end. But it gave that awful brother power over her. There was no one to control him now. And I was truly frightened for her."

Mary couldn't help but feel for the girl. "Do you know what happened next?"

"I saw her one more time," Ms Thorn said. "And... are you sure you need to talk to her?"

"I wouldn't ask if it wasn't really important," Mary said.

"Then you might want to check out West Midlands Science College in Birmingham. She told me she was applying and that there was a distant relative that she could stay with until she could afford to rent somewhere. She wasn't going to tell Michael or Joyce. She was going to escape."

"And did she?"

Now a smile brightened Ms Thorn's face. "She sent me a copy of her graduation photo in the post."

"Can you send me that over?"

"Sure."

Mary gave the woman her email address and hung up the phone. There was a ray of light in the darkness, she thought, if Katie Lynford had managed to escape her family. Now Mary just had to make sure the past didn't come back to haunt her.

At that moment the doorbell rang and the kids piled in. There was a flurry of hugs and kisses and squeals of laughter as the kids fought their way upstairs to dump their stuff. Matt and Stephanie followed behind them.

"I've got loads of washing for you, I'm afraid," Matt said, dragging two black bags through the door. "The washing machine in the rental packed in."

"No problem," Mary said, although her heart sank a little. "Just take it through the back."

"I hope you didn't miss them too much," Stephanie said. Mary was a little pleased to see that the woman looked exhausted.

"Were they well-behaved for you?" Mary asked.

"Oh, little angels." Stephanie replied. Mary noticed that she had what looked like crayon residue on her suede boots.

"You don't have to lie," Mary said. "I know what they're like."

"Well, all right, maybe it was a bit of a challenge. But the cuddles were lovely, even though it was a bit noisy. And Johnny managed to wee in a plant pot so I don't think we'll get our deposit back. Overall it was lovely, but…"

"But you'll be happy to get back to the peace and quiet of your own house?"

Stephanie giggled, her hand in front of her mouth. "Maybe just a little bit. But we did have a lot of fun. Matt's talking about splitting the Easter holidays with you next time. Only if you're up for it, of course."

Mary thought of a whole week free to hang out with Walker and enjoy the silence. Then Lauren ran down the stairs and wrapped herself around Mary's legs.

"I missed you mummy," she said.

"Maybe just a couple of days at Easter," Mary replied. "But thank you for the offer."

Chapter 40: Walker

"We've found Katie Lynford," Macleod said, bursting into the office like an excited puppy.

"How did you find her," Walker said, a little peeved as he had been hoping to be the one to track her down.

"She found us. She saw the press release about Joyce's death and she got in touch. She's getting the train up from Birmingham and she's going to be here this evening. Walker, will you call her and arrange an interview."

This felt like an olive branch from Macleod. "Of course," Walker said, taking the number from him.

He put the call through straight away, but when he got hold of Katie Lynford, she explained that she couldn't meet him straight off the train.

"I've already agreed to another interview, but I could probably fit you in an hour later?"

Walker had a funny feeling he knew the answer, but he had to ask the question: "Who is your other interview with."

"Oh, a nice lady from a detective agency. She was the one who tracked me down in the first place."

"Her name wouldn't be Mary Plunkett, by any chance?"

"You know her? Good, that makes things a bit less awkward."

He wasn't sure about that. "Let me talk to Mary, we might be able to do the interview together. It might save you from having to give the same answers twice."

"All right," Katie said and they ended the call.

Walker decided it was probably best not to let Macleod know that he would be sharing his interview with a member of the WWC. He filled the rest of the time by making sure all his paperwork was up-to-date. He resisted the urge to get Phil Higgins to fix all the mistakes he had made, and was actually pleased to see that the Constable was chatting with a couple of other officers about when they discovered the body. Finding a murder victim as a probationer seemed to be giving him some much-needed street cred.

While he was working he sent a series of text messages explaining to Mary that he would like to join her in interviewing Katie Lynford. Mary reacted in the way that he thought she just might.

Haha, I'll let you tag along!

You can be Toto to my Lone Ranger

Robin to my Batman

The weird bird-winged Brian Blessed to my Flash Gordon

And so it continued until Walker met her at the station.

"Katie is due in around fifteen minutes," Mary said.

"Will we go get her on the platform?"

"Why don't we wait in the station coffee shop? Let her get her breath first. It's got to be a heavy day, finding out her sister is dead and now having to speak to both of us."

Walker was happy to go along with this plan, even if it meant he did have to buy Mary a cinnamon swirl and some sort of gross caramel-syrup whipped cream drink.

When Katie Lynford walked in, Walker was pleasantly surprised. Mary had filled him in on the woman's miserable childhood and somehow he was expecting that to show. But she looked smart, wearing woollen trousers, a black raincoat and neat hair tied back in a bun.

"Can I get you a drink?" Walker asked and when she said she would have an Americano he took the opportunity to let Mary soothe her nerves before the interview started.

By the time he got back, they were chatting about Katie's job as a technician specialising in STEM subjects in secondary school.

"I loved science ever since I was at school," Katie told them.

"Ms Thorn told me that," Mary said. "When I asked her about you, she said you had a talent for it."

"You talked to Annabel Thorn? How is she doing?"

"Good."

They all fell silent for a few seconds. "I suppose you were asking Annabel about my school days," Katie said, hunching over her drink.

"Yes. I hope you don't think I was being intrusive. You see, we were trying to find out where you went. And I guess I wanted to know what life was like for you back then. So that I could try and make sense of what happened."

Katie nodded. "I get that. And you were looking for me before Joyce died, right?"

Mary shared a look with Walker. "I was. You see, we were looking into the death of your stepmother, Mrs Bute."

A shudder passed through the woman. "I don't like to think about that woman. Besides, it was a long time ago."

"That's why the police asked my firm to investigate. Because it wasn't an active case. But now that Joyce has been killed, the police are investigating everything that happened in the past."

"I suppose I was stupid to think I'd escaped it all," Katie said.

"What we would like," Walker said, "is to speak to Michael Bute."

Now the woman looked really uncomfortable. "I haven't seen him in years. Thank God."

Mary leaned forward and touched the woman's hand. "I don't know how to tell you this, but we're wondering if your stepbrother might have been involved with Joyce's death."

Katie tilted her head to one side. "Well, of course he was."

Walker blinked. "Sorry, what did you say?"

"Who else would kill her? Of course it was Michael."

"Oh. Do you have some sort of evidence to show that?"

"Not exactly. Only the evidence of my own brain. Michael Bute is a killer. Who else could have murdered Joyce?"

"How do you know that?" Mary asked.

Katie's voice cracked with emotion. "I think he killed my father."

This was not quite what Walker had been expecting. "You mean... Joe Lynford?"

"That's right. He left one day and never came back. Elizabeth said he had run off with another woman. She was hysterical. But Michael stayed really quiet. And I just knew."

"Why would he kill your dad?" Mary asked. "I thought he liked him."

"He did, at first. It was like... if it was someone on a date, you would say he threw himself at him. Michael wasn't so bad at that point. He was just so desperate to be liked. And at the start my dad treated him like the son he never had. Even took him to a couple of football games. But that was the problem, you see? No one had ever given a crap about Michael, and suddenly Dad is telling him he's the best thing since sliced bread. Of course it all had to go wrong."

"What happened?"

Katie was in her stride now, the words pouring out of her. "Elizabeth, that was what happened. She couldn't stand that Dad was paying attention to Michael. She wanted him all for herself, you see? So she started getting in between them, telling Michael that Dad found him annoying, telling Dad that Michael was only trying to get money out of him… that sort of thing. Again, I wasn't so aware of it at the time, but Joyce told me all about it when I was a bit older. It didn't take long before Michael was getting ignored just like before. And then Dad disappeared. And that's when Michael started hitting Joyce more. Silly things like pinching her arms until he left red bruises, tripping her up when she was heading for the stairs, that sort of thing. The stuff that toddlers do but older kids normally grow out of."

Mary asked the difficult question. "Did he hit you too, Katie? Or anything worse?"

"You're talking about sexual abuse, right? No, as far as I know, he never did that to me or Joyce. I know he was a bit of a creep with the girls at school, but at home it was just hitting. And I never got it that bad. Joyce always protected me."

She sniffed and looked out of the window. Walker was about to ask another question but Mary shook her head so he waited.

"I feel bad for Joyce," Katie said quietly. "She never had much of a life. She managed to get me out of there, but it was like she couldn't see a way out for herself."

"She did escape in the end," Mary said. "She got away from him."

"Not for long, right?"

"We don't know anything for sure right now," Walker felt the need to remind her. "We do want to talk to Michael as a person of interest, but that's all for the moment."

Katie just looked away as if what he had said wasn't worth considering and Mary simply rolled her eyes.

"Do you mind if I head off to my hotel now?" Katie asked. "I'm pretty wiped out."

"Of course not," Walker said. "I'll give you a lift."

They all got up to leave, but Katie paused and took something out of her bag.

"The Detective Inspector I spoke to on the phone, he asked if I had any photos of Michael. And I had this one tucked away. I don't know why I kept it, except it was a nice one of Joyce."

Katie handed over the photograph. It must have been taken not long after Mrs Bute's death. There was Joyce, with her arm around Katie and next to them, grinning for the camera was a tall man with a hint of a belly.

"He… do you know, he almost looks familiar," Mary said, squinting at the photograph.

"What do you mean?"

"I mean that I've seen him before. I've met Michael Bute."

Chapter 41: Bernie

Lucas Duncan looked nothing like his photograph. He was tanned, he had cut his hair short and it looked like he had been working out.

"Does it bother you that he looks like he's having the time of his life," Liz muttered, "while his wife and child are living in misery?"

"With a man of his morals, they're probably better off without him."

They had ended up ordering a mediocre pizza to share while they worked out how to approach the man behind the bar. Isioma was happily chewing on her crust and babbling to the waitress.

As it turned out, the perfect opportunity to meet Lucas presented itself almost immediately. While they were chatting, Isioma reached out of her high chair for a final piece of crust and knocked Liz's glass of Sangria off the table, shattering it in spectacular fashion and splattering pink liquid to a ten-foot radius.

"I'm so sorry," Liz said to the waitress, helping the woman mop up the liquid on the table with some kitchen roll. Meanwhile, Bernie was checking to make sure that no glass had gone anywhere near the baby. Once a nurse, always a nurse.

"At least she's cute," the waitress said, giving Isioma a tickle under her chin.

"Need a hand," a male voice said and Bernie looked up to see that Lucas had arrived with a brush and pan.

"Yes please," she said in the sort of sickly-sweet voice that would make anyone who knew her start backing away to a safe distance.

"What a cute baby," he said as he finished sweeping the glass from the floor.

While Liz beamed, momentarily forgetting who was speaking to them, Bernie leaned forward and gripped his arm.

"Remind you of Marco? He would have been about the same age when you abandoned him and ran off to serve undercooked pizza, right?"

Lucas started to turn red from his collarbone to his forehead. "What the... Who are you?"

"Your worst nightmare," Bernie hissed, only realising that she might have got a little carried away when Liz kicked her on the shin.

"We're private detectives," Liz explained. "We'd like to have a word with you."

Beads of sweat trickled down his temples. "I'm working right now but... I guess I could take a break. Could we sit outside? I don't want the other staff members to hear."

Bernie rolled her eyes but she agreed. The rain had stopped at least and there was a small kid's sandpit to keep Issy occupied.

By the time Lucas came out to join them, he had calmed his nerves. By the smell, Bernie suspected that he had had the help of some clear spirits.

"I can't stay long," he said, glancing back to the bar.

"You've been missing for eighteen months," Liz reminded him. "I reckon you can give us a few minutes."

"It's Fiona that sent you, I suppose."

"That's right. We're a private investigation firm and she asked us to find out what happened to you."

"I didn't think she would still be looking for me," Lucas said, sipping on his beer. "I thought she'd have moved on long ago."

"She called us in to investigate your disappearance. And before that she reported it to the police."

"The police?" Now Lucas looked a bit more concerned. "They're not sniffing about are they?"

"No. Her mother told them to drop it."

"That's good."

Bernie couldn't resist. "Your son is doing just fine, by the way."

This time Liz didn't kick her and Bernie could tell she had been itching to say the same thing.

"Aye, I'm sure he is," Lucas said, oblivious to the wave of female hatred heading his way. "You probably think I'm a loser for not getting in touch."

"I was thinking of other words, but yes."

"I thought a clean break would be better. It's not like I'm just up the road. He needs a dad who's around, not in another country."

"At the moment he doesn't have a dad at all."

"He's better off without me."

Bernie could feel her temper rising but she needed to keep going.

"Why don't you tell us what happened? Why did you leave?"

Lucas dropped his gaze in a way that told Bernie he was about to tell them a lie.

"It was my mental health, you know? I just needed a change of scene. And I knew that I was just bringing Fiona down. So I headed over here and my cousin got me a job. I meant to call, I just felt too bad about everything."

"Bull crap," Liz said, leaning across the table. "I have a friend who is really good with bank accounts. And she can't always give me the details, but I told her I was getting dragged to Spain for a day by a maniac –"

"Hey!"

"Sorry Berns. I told her I was getting dragged to Spain and

was there anything weird about your Spanish bank account. And then she told me that the account was the sort that you can only open with a 'substantial sum' for your initial deposit. So someone gave you a lot of money just as you left Scotland and set up home in Spain."

Lucas groaned and put his head in his hands. "You pretty much know it all then. It was Fiona's mum. Me and Fiona had had a stinking row and Christine came over. She always hated my guts, but this time she was all like 'I'll make you an offer'. And the thing was, I owed some people money in Invergryff. Not the sort of people you want to owe money to either. And I just couldn't say no."

Bernie didn't point out the stupidity of this statement.

"How much?" Liz asked.

"Thirty grand."

In the silence Bernie watched Issy trying to eat sand.

"Thirty grand to give up your family," Bernie said.

Now Lucas's eyes were tearing up, but she didn't have any sympathy for him. She knew that he wasn't crying over Fiona and Marco. He was only crying for himself.

Chapter 42: Liz

The night in the airport hotel hadn't been as bad as Liz had imagined, mainly because they were all so tired that they had fallen asleep immediately, Isioma curled up on the bed next to her. The flight back was best forgotten, with both her and Bernie snapping at each other as their exhaustion started to show. By mutual agreement, they got separate taxis home and after she handed Isioma over to her dad Liz had gone for a blissful two hour nap.

Liz didn't think you could get jet lag when coming back from a country that was only three hours away, but when she woke up she was feeling pretty damn terrible. Two flights in not much more than a day will do that to a person. She popped a couple of painkillers and drank two cups of fancy coffee. She definitely preferred the old blend to whatever Dave had bought recently. It had a weird root vegetable aftertaste. Still, the caffeine did its job and by the time she set off to visit Fiona Duncan, she was feeling mostly awake.

When Liz got to Fiona's flat, she was surprised to see that there was already someone waiting outside. Roxanne Duncan stood clutching a parcel in her arms and looking decidedly nervous.

"I shouldn't have come here," Roxanne said. "I've not even rung the bell. Maybe I should just go." She was wearing a thin cardigan that she wrapped around her chest as tightly as she could.

"You wanted to see Marco?"

Roxanne bit her lip. "I thought… well, I brought him a wee present. I don't know what he's into, but all wee boys like cars, don't they?"

"They do," Liz nodded.

"So I thought, maybe… it was a stupid idea. She won't let me in." The woman looked so wretched that Liz couldn't fight an urge to help her out.

"Actually, I think she could do with some support," Liz said. "I'm about to give her some crappy news."

For a moment, Liz thought Roxanne was about to bolt down the stairs. Then she squared her shoulders and rang the bell.

Fiona's face when she opened the door went from shock to… well, a bit more shock.

"Roxanne, what a surprise," Fiona said.

Roxanne was so overcome by the social awkwardness of the situation that she just thrust a wrapped parcel into Fiona's arms.

"For the baby," she grunted.

"Oh." Fiona stared at them. "I guess you better both come in, then. Tea all around?"

Five minutes later they were sat in what wasn't exactly a friendly atmosphere, but not a hostile one either. Marco was lying on his stomach, happily pushing his new car up and down the carpet. Roxanne looked like she was going to burst into tears at any moment, and Fiona was dealing with the social anxiety by faffing around with drinks and snacks for everyone.

"That's lovely, thanks," Roxanne said when she took a brown sticky object from the tray that Fiona offered her.

"It's a vegan cupcake," Fiona said. "I'm not sure I got the icing quite right."

"Mmn," Roxanne said, although her expression was less enthusiastic. Liz had to hide a smile. She had no problem bolting down the depressing cake. She had eaten enough of Bernie's raw protein bites to be able to eat anything.

Liz swallowed the last bite of her cake and decided she couldn't put it off any longer.

"We found Lucas," she said.

Fiona hissed in a breath. "Where?"

"In Spain. He's working in a bar over there."

"He's... he's not dead? Or married to someone else?" Fiona's face didn't suggest which of these would have been worse.

"No. He's definitely alive. I don't know if he's seeing anyone or not."

"Why hasn't he been in touch?" It was Roxanne asking this time. "With any one of us?"

Liz cleared her throat. "I'm sorry to have to tell you this, Fiona, but it turns out that your parents offered Lucas some money to leave Scotland. He's working over in Spain, on the Costa del Sol. We have an address for him."

"Mum and Dad gave him money? How much?"

"Thirty grand."

There was silence in the room, apart from Marco's engine noises. None of the women looked at each other, but they were all thinking the same thing. Thirty grand wasn't much to give up your wife and child.

"He always was a bit of a tosser," Roxanne said, breaking the silence.

Fiona had pressed her lips together, as if frightened by what she might say.

"I'm sorry that this isn't the outcome you were hoping for," Liz said, aware that her words weren't going to be any comfort. "But at least you know now."

"Yeah."

"I'd better be off," Liz said, feeling terrible. "I'll be in touch over email, okay?"

Fiona nodded. Roxanne got up as well and started to put on her coat.

"No, please don't go," Fiona said, grabbing Roxanne's arm. "Sorry, it's just… Well, I was thinking you might want to stay for a bit. Have some lunch. Marco doesn't have any other aunties you see, so…"

Liz held her breath.

"All right," Roxanne said, easing back onto the sofa. "Why not?"

Feeling a little lighter, Liz left the flat and closed the door behind her. All that remained now was to finish up the file and send Fiona Duncan the bill. Along with the address in Spain for Lucas so that she could claim back-dated child support payments, of course. That might prove rather more than what the WWC had charged her. Maybe not a happy ending, but an ending at least.

Chapter 43: Mary

The caravan park was just as depressing on Mary's second visit. But this time she wasn't worried about the run-down surroundings. She only wanted to know if the man they had spent the last week searching for was still there.

Mary would have loved to go and confront him herself. She was pretty sure that she wouldn't scare Michael Bute off if he saw her. But she had decided that it was wise to alert the police that there was a possible murderer on the loose.

"And you reckon this guy, Bill Stewart, is Michael Bute?" DI Macleod asked her for the third time that morning.

"Yes," Mary said, although with each passing hour she was less sure. She had stared at the photograph that Katie had given them for ages and the resemblance to the guy who worked at the caravan park had to be more than a coincidence, didn't it?

She glanced over at Walker who was in the back of the car making notes. If she was wrong about this, not only would Mary make the WWC look like idiots, but Walker would be made to look like a fool as well.

Macleod and Walker discussed the arrest. It was all a bit thrilling. They had printed off aerial photos of the caravan park. The site was due to open at 11am, and the plan was to surprise their suspect bang on eleven. Along with the car that she was sharing with Macleod, Walker and Constable Higgins, there was a police van with another four officers inside. The butterflies in Mary's stomach had turned into angry stomping gremlins. There was so much pressure to get this right.

Just before eleven, Macleod got on the radio and they proceeded to the campsite. There was only one entrance, so they were hoping that there was no way that Bute could escape.

Mary chewed on her thumb as Macleod drove up to the reception building. The police van would follow in five minutes as it wasn't exactly discrete. Macleod pulled on the handbrake and parked up and for a moment they sat in silence. Then everyone moved.

"You go around the back," Macleod said to Higgins as they got out of the car.

The Constable nodded and ducked low as he ran past the windows, disappearing into the trees behind reception.

"You stay here and don't move a muscle," Walker told her.

"Noted," Mary said, and for once she had no desire to challenge him.

Walker and Macleod headed into the building. There was a low murmur of voices, then a shout.

"He's gone out the back!" Walker yelled.

Mary took a few steps toward the building, then stopped. What was she going to do, grab the man as he went past? He was twice her size and a murderer to boot. Then she heard grunts, a shout and some choice language from the other side of the building.

"I've got him," Phil Higgins called out. "He clocked me one on the nose so you can put him down for resisting arrest as well." The Constable emerged from the back of the building, dragging a man in handcuffs. When Mary got a good look at Higgins she could see he was already sporting the beginnings of a shiner on his right eye.

Michael Bute looked a bit dishevelled by the tussle, but otherwise he didn't seem upset. He was even smiling. It creeped her out.

"Congratulations," Walker said when he walked over to her. "You were right."

"Yeah, I guess I was."

"Why aren't you happier? You caught the murderer. Bernie is going to be over the moon."

"He was right there all along, right under our noses," Mary replied. "If I'd worked it out a little faster then his sister would still be alive."

"You weren't to know," Walker said.

"Wasn't I? I talked to the guy for God's sake. I thought I was so clever telling him I was looking for someone to inherit, he must have seen right through me. God damn it!"

Mary couldn't resist walking towards the van where they were shutting Bute into the back, shrugging off Walker as he tried to stop her.

"Why did you kill your sister?" Mary asked the man in handcuffs.

Michael Bute looked straight at her.

"No comment," he said and then the man gave her a lazy grin.

Mary felt the hairs on the back of her neck stand up as they put Bute into the van. She had met murderers before, but this was the first time she felt like she had faced someone truly evil.

"I just hope we've got enough to charge him," Walker said, coming over to stand next to her.

"What do you mean? He clearly killed his sister, along with his mother and most likely his step-father too."

"But where's the proof for it all?"

"Katie Lynford will testify."

"That girl is a bag of nerves. A defence lawyer will tear her to pieces on the stand."

"But… but…" Mary wanted to say that it wasn't fair, because it wasn't. They had done all that work to find out who killed Mrs Bute and now it seemed to be slipping away.

The patrol car pulled away from the reception and Mary watched it go. She had the horrible feeling that Bute was watching her right back, laughing at her.

"He's not going to say a word," Walker repeated.

"He's killed a whole bunch of people and he's just going to sit there and not say anything?"

Walker sighed. "Look, I know on the telly people always confess and Columbo or whoever is in the whodunit gets a lovely, wrapping it all up confession from the murderer, but in real life that rarely happens. Think about it: why would you say 'yes I did it' if you're hoping to get away with it?"

"Columbo is a howdunit."

"What?"

"It's not a whodunit. It's a howdunit. Because you already know the murderer at the start, so you're just watching to find out why and how they did the murder. And how Columbo is going to solve it."

As she was talking, a van was turning into the caravan park. It had some sort of green logo on the back. Mary watched it glumly. Probably someone looking for a cheap place to stay, never knowing like all the rest that the guy running the place was a multiple murderer.

"Wait a minute, I know that truck."

Mary rushed over to meet it, Walker just managing to keep pace with her.

"Is this someone involved in the case?" he said while they ran.

"If you had asked me ten minutes ago I would have said no," Mary replied. "But now I'm not so sure."

The truck pulled up at the front and a tanned woman got out.

She was carrying a plant, something small with little white flowers. The sort of thing you would give to someone as a gift. She walked up to the front of the building, saw the police constable standing outside and paused.

Mary caught up with her just as she was heading back to her truck. "Hello Patricia. Are you here to sell some gnomes?"

For a minute Patricia Humphreys said nothing. Then she burst into tears.

Chapter 44: Walker

Patricia Humphreys was a sorry-looking creature. Her tanned skin had turned a yellowy colour under the harsh lights of the police station interview room. One of her legs was jittery while she sat on the plastic chair. Opposite her were Superintendent MacKinnon and Detective Inspector Macleod, who had kindly allowed the members of the WWC to watch from the other side of the two-way mirror. Walker was sort of wishing he hadn't been so generous.

"Are you sure she can't see us," Mary said, waving her hand in front of the mirror.

Phil Higgins let out a cough that might have been disguising a laugh.

"She can't see you," Bernie said, although Walker had noticed her ducking as well when the suspect had walked into the room. The members of the WWC were buzzing with excitement and he couldn't blame them. Patricia Humphreys was their best chance at getting a solid conviction for Michael Bute. They had tried to interview Bute an hour ago, but he had 'no commented' his way through the whole thing. The man hadn't got away with the most terrible of crimes for years by being stupid.

"I'm surprised Macleod didn't have you in the interview with them," Bernie said in a somewhat critical tone.

"Humphreys is an elected official so they wanted senior ranks only," Walker explained.

"Makes sense. Considering what a disaster this case has been for the police, they probably need to limit the damage."

Walker was just thinking of a retort when the Superintendent gestured to Macleod to start the tape and the interview began. Once they had all identified themselves for the tape, Macleod started to ask the woman about Michael Bute.

"Are you aware that Bill Stewart was formerly known by the name Michael Bute?"

Patricia looked terrified, but she managed a nod.

"Could you please speak out loud for the tape?"

"Yes," she said. "But I only found that out this week. Before then I thought that Bill was his real name."

"She might be telling the truth," Mary whispered. "She didn't seem like the type who would be involved in anything dodgy."

"You don't have to whisper," Walker said. "They can't hear you."

"Okay," Mary said, still whispering.

Back in the interview room, Patricia Humphreys had paused to compose herself and was now sipping at a plastic cup of water.

"Why don't you tell us what your relationship was to Michael Bute?"

"I've been seeing Bill… Michael, I guess for years. Maybe

three years, on and off. It's never been very serious. After my divorce, I guess I was just a bit lonely, and Bill was one of the few guys to pay attention to me. And he didn't want any commitment which was perfect for me. I didn't want another marriage and he wanted... well, I guess he wanted a weekly shag, if I'm being honest."

Walker didn't let his eyes wander to the members of the WWC to see what they thought of this confession, but he did hear Bernie snigger.

"And you didn't realise that he was living under an assumed name?"

"Why would I?" Patricia blew her nose. "Everyone knew him as Bill. When he told me... when it all came out I asked him if no one recognised him from when he was here before, but he just said that Michael Bute kept to himself. And it was true. I never met him back then, even though I knew his sister a little. He said he was looking for a chance to start again."

"Did he tell you why he wanted this 'new start'?"

"Like I said, it only came out a few days ago. He said he'd been in trouble for fraud – he mentioned some old lady's will or something – so he wanted a fresh start. I guess I wasn't too happy that he had been lying to me, but I didn't know anything about anyone getting killed."

"Why did he tell you anything?"

"He was acting weird. He started talking about leaving Invergryff, saying it was time to move on. I guess... well, I was jealous, thought he might have been seeing someone else. So eventually he said the police might be looking for him and he would have to lie low for a while."

"And you didn't think that was the point to come and speak to us," the Superintendent said.

"He blackmailed me!" Patricia wailed. "He said that if I didn't protect him, he would tell everyone that I had been dating a fraud."

"A fraud?"

"He said that the police wanted him for stealing some money, remember. I didn't realise… he never mentioned murder, for God's sake."

"And when you heard that Joyce Bute was dead, that didn't change your mind?"

Patricia Humphreys hugged her arms across her chest. "I still thought he was Bill Stewart, remember? I didn't connect him with her death, although I did think it weird that she died right after I'd been talking about her."

"So how did you find out his real identity?"

"Two days ago I came up to see him and he had the local paper on the counter. I noticed it, because he wasn't exactly a reader, you know? And he had this weird look on his face and there on the front page was the article about Joyce's death. And then I saw that behind him were three other papers, all for that day. Like he needed to read them all."

"I started freaking out. He realised and he grabbed my arm. So hard he left bruises, see?" She pulled up her sleeve to show the marks. "He told me that he was Joyce's brother, Michael. That Joyce had been threatening him, making up stories about him. He had gone round to see her and they argued. She fell."

There were snorts of derision at this from the ladies of the WWC, but Walker kept his eyes on the interview room.

"And you didn't go to the police at this point?"

"I was scared. He told me he was leaving and I guess I thought that that would solve the problem. I was worried that if I said anything, he might hurt me too. I was going to come and tell you all about it once he was out of the way."

"You should have reported the crime, Ms Humphreys," Macleod said. "It is very serious to conceal a murder."

"I know. I just didn't have another choice."

"You assisted Mr Bute in covering his tracks, didn't you?"

"I tried to stay out of it as much as possible, but he made me make a phone call. I told that nice investigator lady with the terrible clothes that he had moved to London. He made me say it!"

Walker didn't look at Mary to see how that comment had gone down, but he could imagine she wouldn't be too impressed.

Patricia Humphreys had broken down in tears now and the officers in the interview room were wrapping things up.

"You reckon we'll get our conviction?" Mary asked him.

"I think a local councillor will make an excellent witness," Walker replied. "We've got a decent chance."

The door opened and DI Macleod walked in, looking satisfied with his morning's work.

"Hello, Detective Inspector," Bernie said. The smugness and 'I told you so' was radiating from her like invisible lightning.

"I think I owe you an apology, Mrs Paterson," Macleod said. "I should have trusted that your organisation would come up with a result."

"That's right," Bernie said, "and another thing –"

Like a pair of synchronised swimmers, both Liz and Mary shot out an arm and pinched Bernie on the elbows.

"Ouch!"

"We're so glad we could help you reach a satisfactory conclusion on this case," Liz said, raising her voice so that it reached over Bernie's grumbles.

"We'd love it if you would consider us for other cases," Mary added.

"I'll certainly think about it," Macleod replied.

"I think we'll head home now," Liz said, strong-arming Bernie towards the door. Mary followed behind them and they headed along the corridor towards the exit.

Those left in the room could hear the snippets of conversation as the door closed including 'we saved his arse' and 'pompous old windbag'.

Walker glanced at Macleod who had set his jaw and was pretending he couldn't hear a thing.

"It looks like we've got a strong case for the Procurator Fiscal," Walker said, trying to break the ice.

"Yes. Patricia Humphreys should prove a good witness for the prosecution. I'm going to charge Bute with his sister's murder and his mother's. And I want to follow up with Katie Lynford and see if we can add the murder of Joe Lynford to the list of charges."

"Sounds good," Walker said. "Mind if I go and speak to Mary?"

Macleod waved him off, his head already bent over the paperwork.

"You know, you're pretty good at this investigating business," Walker said when he caught up to his girlfriend in the car park. Liz had already bundled Bernie into her car and driven away before the woman could cause any trouble.

"So people kept telling me," Mary said, giving him a quick smile. "Bernie was asking again if I wanted to go full time with the WWC."

"Well, why don't you?"

She sighed. "I don't know."

"Maybe the reason you haven't said to Bernie you'll do more hours is that you don't think you're good enough. I mean, you keep saying that you're just a part-timer, or just the admin assistant. But Bernie wants you to come on board as a full partner, doesn't she?"

"Yes."

"And why would you say no, unless there's a part of you that thinks you're not worth it? But Bernie clearly thinks you can handle it. And so do I."

Mary shuffled her feet. "It's going to be hard. I'll have to sort out the kids and school and work out how I'm going to fit everything in."

"It might not be the easy option," Walker agreed, "but what if it's what you're meant to do? I don't want to get all spiritual or anything, you know it's not my thing, but watching you work for the WWC, it just seems like the perfect fit. Today a murderer is going to jail that wouldn't be if you hadn't caught him. And I think in life when something like that happens, you have to go for it."

Mary stroked his stubbly chin. "Is that how you feel about me?"

"Absolutely," Walker smiled, bending to kiss her. "I never meant to fall for someone who actually thinks that Trek is better than Wars, but it happened. And I wouldn't change it. You're really good at this investigation business. I reckon you should go all in with the WWC. Otherwise, you'll always regret it."

Epilogue: Valentine's Day

Invergryff's nicest Spanish restaurant was absolutely heaving on Valentine's Day. The candles on the table were fluttering with the volume of conversation and the smell of 'second-cheapest-on-the-menu' wine was almost overpowering.

"It's busy, isn't it?" Mary said, raising her voice above the sound of the people from the tables around them.

Walker nodded. He was looking around at all the people like a cat in a room of strangers. She had forgotten that crowds made him nervous. It was his army background, not helped by his cop instincts which meant he was always waiting for someone to kick off.

"Are you having a good time?" Mary asked him.

"Of course," he lied. "I thought we were going to have a games night? And you were going to make those marshmallow things on the barbeque with the kids."

"Smores. Yeah, but that's not as exciting as… this," Mary said.

"I think it is," Walker said, reaching over to squeeze her hand and nudging some of his red wine onto the table. "Sorry, I'll clean it up."

A splash of red had landed on her dress, but Mary ignored it. She was determined to have a great night, even if someone at the next table seemed to be breaking up with their husband.

"It's nice to spend time just us, isn't it?" Mary said, trying to talk over the life-changing argument happening nearby.

"Yeah."

"I mean, the kids are amazing, but it's not like we get to have a proper chat or anything."

"Oh, I wasn't thinking of the kids," Walker replied. "I was thinking of Bernie and Macleod and all the rest. It is nice to spend some time together without people getting murdered."

"It's kind of our jobs though, isn't it? I mean, it's not just a part time thing anymore now that I'm going to be a full partner in the WWC."

"I think it's a great idea," Walker grinned.

"Really? You think I should go for it?"

"You've found something you're really good at. I know you never planned for this, but you've clearly got a talent for investigation. I mean, if you were in the force you would be a prime candidate for CID."

"I don't think I'd pass the fitness test," Mary giggled. "Or the attitude test for that matter."

At the next table, the woman stood up and stormed out of the room. The man legged it after her.

"Thank goodness for that," Walker said. "I was worried she was going to thump him one and then I'd have to arrest them both for affray."

"That would have been quite sexy though," Mary said.

"Really?"

"Totally."

They sipped their respective drinks.

"Did you hear that they found Joe Lynford's body?" Walker asked.

"Yes. One of Bernie's sisters heard it from a guy who does the hedge trimming at the estate next to the caravan park."

"Of course she did."

"I heard that he buried him right next to the tennis courts. No wonder they looked rundown. He wouldn't have wanted anyone going near them.

Walker nodded. "We think that's why he kept going back there. To keep an eye on the place, make sure no one had disturbed his homemade grave. And then eventually he took the opportunity to change his name and start working there. No one realised who he was, they had such a high turnover of staff there was no one left from the time that Michael and Joyce Bute lived there. And so Bill Stewart was born."

She was just about to ask him for some details about Joe Lynford's death when her phone started to ring.

"Sorry, it's the babysitter." Mary answered the phone only to hear Liz's voice was rather strained.

"Please don't panic," her friend said.

"Oh god," Mary felt her heart thump. "What's happened?"

"Everyone is okay. But we are at the hospital."

Mary let out a groan. "Who's hurt?"

"Johnny and Peter had an argument about who had the biggest head. And apparently the best way to solve that is to stick your head through the bannisters."

"They got stuck?"

"Not on that one. But after that they tried the baby gate. God knows how Johnny got into it, but we couldn't get him out. So we've had to dismantle it and bring it with us to A&E. He's all right, but everyone keeps laughing at him so it's his pride that's hurt more than anything. But he's asking for his mum so I thought I better call."

"I'll head right over."

"Thanks. And do you think Walker would mind going over to my place? I've had to leave Dave with the rest of the kids and I think he's having a breakdown. He's locked himself in the bathroom ever since they found the water pistols."

"Of course."

"Sorry to ruin your dinner."

"Don't worry about it," Mary said. She clicked off the call and gave Walker an apologetic look.

"Time to go?" he asked.

"Yes. Sorry."

"Don't be," Walker replied.

"Bloody hell, we almost managed a full meal," Mary said, putting on her coat. "I'm so sorry that it didn't work out."

"Don't worry, it's just one of those things," Walker said, leading her over to his car.

"One of those things that happens every week or so."

"Yeah, one of them." He kissed her on the forehead. "But I wouldn't want it any other way."

They walked over to the car and got in. Luckily she had decided to drive and not drink, so at least she wouldn't have to get a taxi to the hospital.

"What's that?" Mary asked, realising that Walker was carrying a box which he sat on his knee.

"I asked for dessert to take home," Walker said. "I got us a strawberry cheesecake and a death by chocolate. And I got them to double the portions so the kids can have some too."

"Happy Valentine's Day," Mary said, kissing him just before he put the key in the ignition.

"You too," Walker replied.

Afterword

Thank you for reading the latest novel in the Wronged Women's Co-operative series. I had so much fun writing this one. Much more fun than a last minute two-day holiday to Spain in the company of Bernie Paterson, that's for sure!

The next novel in the series, *Multi Level Murder,* is available to order now.

Printed in Great Britain
by Amazon